"I like tha[t],"
Cady whispered

"All my life I've never been held enough, or touched enough."

Luke's firm, gentle hand stroked her hair, her skin, and he held her close against his naked warmth. "Ah," he said softly, "what luck. I want to touch you enough for a lifetime."

She needed his warmth. She needed everything he had to offer, and the sudden realization caused a flood of nameless longing.

He kissed away her tears. "All right," he whispered soothingly. "It's all right." And when her sobs subsided he knew the child had been satisfied.

Then he began to touch the woman. . . .

Dear Reader,

We at Harlequin are extremely proud to introduce
our new series, **HARLEQUIN TEMPTATION**.
Romance publishing today is exciting, expanding
and innovative. We have responded to the ever-
changing demands of you, the reader, by creating
this new, more sensuous series. Between the covers
of each **HARLEQUIN TEMPTATION** you will find
an irresistible story to stimulate your imagination
and warm your heart.

Styles in romance change, and these highly
sensuous stories may not be to every reader's taste.
But Harlequin continues its commitment to
satisfy all your romance-reading needs with
books of the highest quality. Our sincerest wish is
that **HARLEQUIN TEMPTATION** will bring you
many hours of pleasurable reading.

THE EDITORS

U.S.
HARLEQUIN TEMPTATION
2504 WEST SOUTHERN AVE.
TEMPE, ARIZONA
85282

CAN.
HARLEQUIN TEMPTATION
P.O. BOX 2800
POSTAL STATION "A"
WILLOWDALE, ONTARIO
M2N 5T5

The Forever Kind

ALEXANDRA SELLERS

Harlequin Books

TORONTO • NEW YORK • LONDON
AMSTERDAM • PARIS • SYDNEY • HAMBURG
STOCKHOLM • ATHENS • TOKYO • MILAN

for
Joy
Gordon
Margaret
and
Donna

———————————◆———————————

The quote on page 145 is from "Like a Rolling Stone."
Words and music by Bob Dylan. © 1945 Warner Bros. Inc.
All rights reserved. Used by permission.

Published April 1984

ISBN 0-373-25106-8

Printed in Canada

PROLOGUE

CADY LAY ON THE SOFA, curled into it, her unprotected
back to the room. In her restless sleep she heard the
footsteps, coming from a distance, closer and closer.
Her dream was a nightmare of panic: she knew that
some horror would touch her if she let the walker reach
her.

Open your eyes! she commanded herself, feeling the
sweat start on her forehead, on her whole body. *Open
your eyes!* That was the only way to stop the footsteps—she had to force open her eyes. From the depths
of sleep she strained to find the muscles that would per-
form that function, strained to make them understand
that this was real, not a dream message.

There. Cady stared at the worn brown corduroy of
the sofa, and the footsteps were silent. She was too ex-
hausted to move, but she knew that the moment her
eyes closed the footsteps would begin again. With an
effort she rolled over onto her back and lay with her
eyes open, staring at the ceiling. The room was filled
with late-afternoon light and the comforting glow that
meant the world outside was covered in snow.

She hadn't had the dream for years. Not since she was
eleven or twelve, when they had finally found her a
foster home where she fit in. Where she felt secure. Up
till then she had had it constantly, waking up night after
night screaming as if all the horsemen of hell were after
her.

Cady made a little noise that might have been a

laugh. No wonder she hadn't fit in in the foster homes. Yet at that one, not the last but the best, she had somehow been accepted, and the nightmare had stopped. For sixteen years she had been free of it, until now. In the past three months it had come more and more often, till now it was as much a part of her life as it had been when she was a child.

Cady swung her legs off the sofa and sat up, her head dropping in exhaustion. What had made her so tired anyway, dropping off like that in the middle of the afternoon?

Her large suitcase sat in the center of the room, and she closed her eyes against the sight. Oh God. Monday, this was Monday. Could she have missed him? Could she have slept right through? Cady glanced at her watch. No, there was time. There was too much time.

The room seemed cold. She switched on a lamp for comfort, then reached for a cigarette and, lighting it, crossed to the window.

The city was covered with a fresh fall of snow. It was a hard winter for Toronto—her first Canadian winter for six years. She had been homesick for this, for four strongly marked seasons; the sight of that heavy white blanket was soothing to her. Not a car in sight, and everything as peaceful as a small town on the prairie.

Cady laughed. She had lived through a hard winter in London once, a winter that had reminded her of home. The English hadn't seemed to know how to live with it. They didn't know, perhaps because it happened to them so rarely, that the white, quiet fall of snow could be one of nature's best gifts. They didn't know the pleasure, the joy that could be found in nature's extremes.

Listen to that quiet. And the smell, the smell of a real winter. She dragged on her cigarette. Night was falling, and suddenly in the window she could see her own face, and behind her, in the softly lighted room, the suitcase. Oh God, why had she ever come home?

Luke. The name was suddenly inside her head, gently resistless, bringing its own pool of anguish that lapped like acid at all the contours of her mind.

No, she told the memory, *I can't think of you now. You aren't part of this, you aren't even part of my life. You never were. I don't want to think of you—not to-night when I'm going off with someone else, and everything I've ever wanted depends on that. I don't want to remember!*

Cady shook her head impatiently. The smoke from her cigarette was making her eyes water, and she squashed the glowing tip against the fading colors of the Union Jack on the cheap bright ashtray beside her. That made the smoke more acrid, and it caught in her nostrils, making her cough.

Smoke....

1

THE SMELL OF WOODSMOKE was pleasant, but when she caught her first whiff of it late on her fourth afternoon in the park, Cady wrinkled her nose in wry disappointment. Her map had shown only one campsite on this tiny lake, and it was too late to portage to the next.

She had seen no one for four days, which was just the way she wanted it. By October Algonquin Park was becoming deserted, with only die-hard outdoorsmen still making treks into the interior. Or someone like herself, Cady thought, someone homesick for the heart of Canada after six years of self-exile.

This was, to her, the heart of Canada. It was the wilderness that made this country different from any other. Other countries were remembered by their cities and skylines, by the man-made trappings that characterized them. But to Cady the sight of red and orange and brown maple leaves against the rarefied blue of the October sky would always be Canada.

She dropped her small canoe at the water's edge and, easing her shoulders free of the straps, lowered the heavy backpack inside. She had chosen a difficult route, considering how little of this kind of thing she had done in the past six years. She moved her shoulders uncomfortably. She was tired and sore. Maybe she would stop here for a couple of days, provided that the people whose woodsmoke she could smell intended to move on in the morning. She had come here to think, after all, not to force herself to the sort of pace that made thinking too much effort.

She pushed the canoe off the small pebbly shore, got inside and began to work the paddle in the cold, clear lake.

It was a small lake. She could see the whole shoreline on one side, but on the other a curve of rocks and trees jutting into the water hid the campsite from her view.

Cady cast a rapid mental eye over the picture of the map of the park she carried in her head. You could make a mistake, sometimes, planning your own route, and find that a place that had taken you four days of hard packing and paddling to reach had been for others a half-day hike from one of the lumber roads. Cady was hoping she hadn't made that kind of mistake, that the smoke she could smell didn't belong to a noisy group of beer-drinking teenagers with a loud radio. If it did, she would paddle by. A stream of some sort ran out of this lake to the next, according to her map. A portage would be necessary at some point along it, but with luck it might be a short portage, one she could make before nightfall. Cady flexed her shoulder muscles gingerly. She wasn't looking forward to that.

It wasn't a noisy group of day-tekkers. The campsite looked pleasant and inviting, with one small orange tent almost camouflaged in the fall colors of the forest and a compact woodsman's fire just where it should be.

A dark-haired man was kneeling at the water's edge filling a pot with water, and it was likely he was alone. Cady made a face. She wished there were a woman with him. She had to make a decision on so little evidence. She could hardly paddle up to him and say, "I'd just like to look in your face to see if you're trustworthy before I decide whether to stop or push on. . . ."

He heard her then, or sensed her presence, and lifted his head attentively, the pot of water in his hand. He looked at her and then glanced west toward the setting sun. She could see by the motion of his shoulders as he looked back at her that he understood the situation and was resigned to it. Resigned, but not happy to have his solitude broken into, and it was that that decided her. That and the muscle in the back of her neck that was screaming for a rest.

With expert paddling, Cady maneuvered the silver canoe up beside the rock he stood on and anchored herself momentarily, pressing the paddle on the rock; and then she blinked and stopped breathing.

The man above her was dark and lean, with a thick thatch of nearly black hair, thick straight black eyebrows and a growth of beard that bespoke several days in the bush. His face was lean and his features strongly marked, and his eyes were a deep, dark blue.

He had stood up as she approached, and now he gazed down at her, unsmiling, with a look of such stunned surprise on his face that she smiled involuntarily and thought, *you feel it too.* She was feeling the strangest sense of rightness, as though not just the past four days but all her life had been a journey through time and space to be at this exact conjunction of hour and latitude. And if she had a coherent thought then, it was: after twenty-eight years, how very odd to have stepped into the pattern of life just here, and just now. She felt the oddest urge to say, "You made it," as though they had appointed this meeting place in some other time, some other realm. The stupidity of that startled her into awareness and brought the heavy weight of logic down to crush the small, quiet understanding telling her that, in spite of everything, she too had made it.

Obedient to that logic, she squinted smilingly up at him and asked, as though that moment of recognition had never happened, "Mind if I share this site for tonight? It's the only one on the lake."

He looked as though he were grateful for the enforced return to the ordinary laws of the universe, the normal

ways of seeing. He grinned impersonally back at her,
clenching his fist more firmly on the handle of the pot he
held at his side. He had spilled more than half of the
water over his foot while they looked at each other, but
they hadn't noticed then and they ignored it now.

"Yes," he said. "I mean, sure. If you pitch your tent
on the other side of the fire—" he gestured with an arm
"—it'll save you making one of your own."

She beached her silver canoe beside his bright yellow
one in a patch where a lot of greenery grew up between
the pebbles of the shore and softened the scrape of stone
on aluminum. Cady wiped her hands on her blue jeans
and unstrapped the tent from her backpack, grateful for
the necessity of small, ordinary tasks that proved the
laws of nature had not changed during the past five
minutes.

She passed him as he was leaning over the campfire,
setting the pot on to boil. "Hungry?" the man called.
"I'm making supper."

Between the fresh air and the exercise, she had had an ex-
cellent appetite for days. She was nearly ravenous now.
"Yes, please!" She wasn't turning down that offer. "My
pack is beside the canoes. Use some of my food, too."

Thank goodness for the settled people of the world,
Cady was thinking as she pitched the small, familiar
tent that six years ago she had left in Thea's basement
locker along with her pack and other items she could
not take with her to England. Cady wasn't settled herself; she was a wanderer. But she liked the fact that Thea
was still in the same apartment six years later; that however quickly Cady moved against it, the background of
her life did not change. To Cady, who had never had a
real home, that was the only security there was.

For no reason whatsoever that she could think of, she
paused during the hammering of a tent peg and turned
to watch the dark stranger by the fire.

You'd be safe, she thought inconsequently. An odd kind of longing swept her, and if she had been forced to put it in words, she would have said, *I wish this moment could last forever. I wish I could hammer in this tent peg for millennia, waiting for that man over there to cook dinner on a fall afternoon, with a campfire crackling in the air....*

Arrested by her stillness, he looked up and met her gaze, and she guarded against the sense of recognition. "Need help?" he asked easily, and Cady bent her head with a short negative shake and resumed her hammering.

If she had been alone, Cady might have stripped off and bathed in the lake before the sun went down, in spite of her hunger. It had been a warm day, and she felt sweaty under the long-sleeve navy turtleneck. And after four days on the trail her hair needed washing. Well, she was definitely due for a rest. Tomorrow—at this site or the next, depending on the dark man's plans—she was going to stop, for a couple of nights at least.

"Ready for dinner?" the man's voice asked behind her as Cady rolled out her sleeping bag inside the expertly pitched tent. She hadn't forgotten much during her years away.

She grinned in appreciation of the appetizing smell emanating from the campfire. "Back in a sec," she said, and ran lightly down to the water's edge to rinse her face and hands in the cold lake.

"What's for dinner?" It was nearly dark now, and when he had finished cooking the man had built up the fire again. Its orange glow was comforting against the night, and it flickered over his face and hair and his lean body, changing his face, or highlighting it somehow, so that she really almost thought she knew him. They looked at each other across the fire, she standing, he sitting. He was wearing a sleeveless down jacket now over

the plaid flannel shirt that was rolled up over strong
forearms.

"Do...do I know you?" she asked, before she could
stop herself.

His gaze was steady in the flickering firelight. Around
them the night deepened.

"I don't know," he returned softly. "Do I know you?"

Well, he might, of course. If he traveled at all he
might have seen something she'd done in London. Cady
winced away from the sudden thought of her career and
its problems. Somehow there was no room to be thinking about something as basically horrible as sleeping
with Miles Davidson to get a film part. It polluted the
atmosphere as surely as if she were dumping a ton of
chemical waste into the tiny lake.

Cady grinned. "Don't think so," she said, and flicked
one long black braid casually over her shoulder, determined to break the mood with matter-of-factness. She
moved around the fire to him. "What's your name?"

"Luke."

"Cady." She flung back the other braid and stuck out
her hand for him to shake. His hand was broad and
lean, like himself, and he took her hand in his with a
small smile that said he understood why she was trying
so hard to establish a natural distance between them.

Immediately she fell under the spell of his smile, and
the handclasp went on and on. When she realized it,
Cady pulled away and used the hand to push up the
long sleeve of her sweater.

"Food!" She sank down onto a rock placed con-
veniently, if a little too close to the stranger, on the
windward side of the fire. "What have you cooked?"

He had unpacked her metal eating utensils, and she
picked them up and looked eagerly into the steaming
saucepan he had placed on the ground between them.

"A packet of my stew mixed with some of your

freeze-dried meat," he told her, as though he were proud to have thought of it. "Cheese, apples and bread." He scooped some of the mixture onto her plate while she inhaled appreciatively, then began to eat.

"Oh, boy," she moaned, feeling she would not be able to eat quickly enough to assuage her hunger. "Delicious!"

"Bread?" he offered after they had spent a couple of minutes silently dedicated to taking the edge off their hunger. He held up a cellophane-wrapped loaf as though he were offering gold, and Cady gurgled in astonished laughter.

"White bread?" she demanded in amazement. "On the trail in Algonquin Park?"

"I can't live without it," Luke confessed. "I carry it on the outside of my pack to prevent crushing and wrap it in three different plastic bags to keep it dry."

Cady laughed outright, set down her plate and stood. "Your hoard is safe from me," she told him, moving over to where her pack lay by the tent. She squatted, unzipped a zipper and rooted around for a moment before straightening up again. As she approached the fire Cady lifted what she was holding to his better view—a loaf of heavy, dark bread. "Stone-ground whole-wheat flour and no preservatives." She grinned. "Try some?"

Luke made a wry face. "I've heard of your kind," he said in dire tones. He clutched the white loaf to his chest. "You want to make the world unsafe for junk-food lovers!"

It seemed funnier than it was, and they laughed more than it deserved, as though any difference between them was to be welcomed for use against the tension that was always there.

But the last word he had said was "lovers," and when the laughter died it remained, hanging in the air between them.

The fire crackled loudly and spat a bright singing spark up into the blackness, and Luke moved to add a log unnecessarily in the middle of the blaze.

They finished dinner, talking quietly about the most impersonal subjects they could find. Politics, which interested neither, died early; poetry, once they discovered a mutual fondness for John Donne, was too dangerous; films were of passionate interest to both. They settled on films. Luke seemed to have a professional knowledge and interest in film, but Cady did not ask him why. Nor did he ask her. The more anonymous they remained, the better—that, too, was tacitly agreed between them.

When the full moon rose they moved on to deeper subjects, religion and the universe and nature. But the moon's light was dangerous, glinting over the water and shaping their faces and bodies and eyes with its magic silver shadows. Luke, who had been lying by the fire while she sat cross-legged, stretched and rolled and got up.

"Got to get some sleep," he said apologetically, brushing off the earth that had adhered to his jeans and down jacket. "I'm leaving early. You?"

"I'm going to stay here for a day or two," Cady said. "But I'm usually up early, so I'll see you in the morning."

In companionable silence they looked after the fire, hoisted their food high on a branch to keep it out of the reach of bears and tidied the little campsite. With the casual tones of distant acquaintances they said goodnight and moved to their tents.

Cady undressed in the darkness, brushed out her long black hair and got ready for bed. When she was finished, dressed in the cream track suit that served her as pajamas, she slid down into her sleeping bag and lay listening to the soft voices of nature at night—and the sounds of movement from Luke's tent.

There was wind on the water, and the rustle of leaves, and the scurry of a night animal. There was the whistle of a long zipper being done up, then a sigh and silence. Luke had settled to sleep.

Cady lay with her arms folded under her head in the darkness, wide awake and staring. She would not settle to sleep for a long time yet. She felt electrified with an energy she did not want to name. Now that there was no more necessity for disguise, she could have taken out the stored memories of the evening and examined the strange, compelling affinity that was between her and Luke. But her mind drew back from those thoughts as from a dangerous abyss.

She sighed and turned over and forced her mind to relax, but sleep wouldn't come. Luke's smiling eyes stared straight into hers, and it was like looking into her own soul. Cady snapped her eyes awake.

A long time later, feeling restless and confined in the small tent, she sat up and slid her sleeping bag silently open, then did the same with the flap of the tent. Slowly, slowly, so as not to wake Luke with the distinctive *zripp* of the large metal zipper.

The moon was high in the sky, silvery white and riding on storm clouds. The wind was increasing, and there might be rain before morning.

The flat smooth earth of the campsite was cold under her feet, but Cady enjoyed the sensation. Slowly, trying not to stub her toes on any pebbles, she made her way down to the water's edge and sat on a large rock. The water was icy, and she quickly pulled out the foot she had experimentally dabbled in the shallows. That was one drawback of autumn camping—no night swimming. Even in the day it was like taking an ice bath, but Cady liked swimming in the cold, fresh-water lakes of Algonquin Park. She could stand temperatures that other people could not, and she would go swimming tomorrow unless the storm clouds building up there brought a change in the Indian summer weather of the past few days.

The clouds began to worry her, and she glanced back at the campsite. If there were a rainstorm she would have a filthy time trying to get a fire going in the morning.

Cady slipped into her tent and felt in her pack for one of the big green garbage bags she always carried on the trail. They were great protectors against rain. Outside again, she dragged the small woodpile in against the dead fire, covered everything with the green plastic and placed stones securely around the perimeter to hold it down.

Now what else? She cast an anxious eye up at the gathering clouds and shivered. How much rain did they carry? She hadn't dug a trench around her tent tonight, but perhaps she ought to have done so. The site was on high ground, but still. . . . Her little trowel, she remembered suddenly, was up in the tree in the food pack. She had put it in with her plate and other utensils for no reason except that they would all be together.

Damn! She cursed that stupidity now. Well, she would just have to get it down, as silently as possible so as not to wake Luke.

He had made a rough pulley with a rope thrown over the branch of a tree and had fixed the end around the wide trunk with a Gordian knot. With chilled fingers she tried again and again, but the knot defied her.

She was getting cold. She ought to get back to bed as soon as possible, and she still had a trench to dig. Maybe Luke's trowel was around someplace. Maybe it was in his tent.

Cady crept silently to the front of his tent, soundlessly slid open the zipper and pulled back the flap. She had expected to see Luke's sleeping face, but instead what met her gaze in the moonlight was the bottom of his sleeping bag. He slept with his head inward. Gingerly Cady felt the floor of the tent along the sides of the bag, but her fingers met nothing but nylon, and on the other side, his hiking boots. There was a movement in the sleeping bag, and she paused, half in and half out of the little tent.

"Luke," she whispered almost soundlessly. If that disturbed him, she would leave. She didn't want to risk waking him.

There was no answer. Biting her lip in silent dismay, Cady crept further into the tent, groping for the touch of metal.

He didn't snore, that was for sure. He didn't even breathe deeply. In fact, there was so little sound from him she could almost believe he was holding his breath.

Cady went still. "Luke?" she breathed softly.

Strong lean arms reached for her in the darkness then, and she was pulled down into a warmth she had been waiting for all her life.

"Oh, Cady," said Luke in her ear. "God knows we tried."

Her breath stopped in her throat. "I— Luke..." she began, as for the second time that night logic struggled against the sweet, pervading sense of rightness that filled her, top to toe. *A trowel*, cried her dulled brain through the misty sea of feeling.

"Luke," she tried again in obedient response, "do you...I need...."

"Yes," whispered Luke in her ear, as gently as the softest of breezes on a warm summer night. "Yes, I do. I'm glad you came, Cady. I'm glad you needed to come."

His mouth was incredibly soft, though it looked so firm. Its warmth against her chilled skin was a miracle as Luke kissed her cheek, the corners of her mouth and then her waiting lips with a gentle tasting and a lack of urgency she found comforting. The arm that wrapped her close against his body moved after a moment, and she heard the noise of the sleeping bag's zipper.

"You're cold," said Luke softly. "Come inside." He half lifted her in against him, then sat up and leaned forward. The sleeping bag fell to his waist and then his hips as he reached for the tent zipper. He moved into a ray of moonlight that pierced a dark cloud, and in the moment before he pulled the zipper down, she saw his naked torso. Black hair curled on his arms and chest and ran down his smooth stomach to disappear under the folds of the sleeping bag.

Then they were shut inside the night and the warmth, and his hair-roughened skin was against her in the darkness.

His hand stroked her hair and scalp with a knowing sureness that made her sigh in fulfillment, and he held her close.

"I like that," she whispered. "All my life I've never been held enough, or touched enough." She had never told anyone that before, but she could say it to Luke, the stranger who had never been a stranger, the man who would disappear with the night. It was safe to confess a weakness, a need to him, that no other man had ever heard.

"Ah," he said softly, "what luck. I want to touch you enough for a lifetime." Then he bent his head, and his kiss moved across her forehead, her eyes, cheeks, throat and lips. His strong hand ran down her arm from shoulder to elbow, and then back up again. His other arm, encircling her back, lifted her throat to his warm gentle mouth, and then his face pressed between her breasts.

"Are you warm enough?" he asked, as his hand moved onto her stomach and slid under the top of her track suit. His skin was so warm against hers, it was like being beside a stove. The more skin she exposed to him, the warmer she would be.

She needed his warmth. She needed everything he had to offer. "Yes," she whispered, nodding against the warm furry chest above her, and he slid the jersey up over her breasts and helped her ease it off.

Cady shivered involuntarily as the night air hit her skin, and then Luke enveloped her totally in his warmth, bending over her and wrapping her securely to his chest.

He kissed her neck at her shoulder, and she shivered again, but not with the cold. She was filled with yearning, drowning with a need of him so strong she did not know how it could ever be filled. It was the need of a lifetime, the nameless longing of twenty-eight empty years.

She felt the tears on her cheeks when his tongue found them, and his lips kissed them away. "All right," whispered Luke. "It's all right."

Nothing frightened him. Not her tears, not her yearning, not the desperate need that she had confessed with words and with her body. She wrapped her arms around his naked warmth and clung and kissed him, shoulders, neck, cheek. His hands wrapped her, pressed her, held her with all the sureness of his own need, and her flesh responded with an ache of fulfillment that tore at her throat until she let it out in a high keening moan like a child's cry.

He touched her again, pressing her stomach, hip, thigh, back and breasts, her face and head with that same strong, sure pressure.

And when her moans subsided and her breathing began to quicken and he knew the child had been satisfied, he began to touch the woman. Now his mouth kissed her full breasts, teased the nipples to hardness. Now she felt an urgency build in him, felt his body prepare for her, demand that she prepare for him.

There was an urgency in her, too, an urgency that rose to the erotic touch of his mouth and hands and hungered for more. When he moved his hand impatiently against the thick jogging trousers she still wore, Cady lifted her hips and moved her legs, eager to help him, eager to be naked against him.

When he raised his body she slid under him, to be enveloped again by him, by his heat. She moved her legs along the outside of his, cradling him in her rounded woman's hips with a kind of pride, and waited.

He smiled at her, a smile she could see in the gloom. "You open to me so freely," he said softly. "That feels so good."

A sudden noisy gust of wind smashed against the tent then, and in the sudden stillness, rain began to patter against the nylon all around them.

She felt safe, safe and protected here in this tiny enclosed space with him. She lifted a hand to his face in the darkness and whispered his name.

He lifted his hips then, and his body demanded entry, and found it; and Cady sighed a long sigh of completion.

The rain and wind beat against the tent in mounting urgency, and it seemed to her that the urgency of nature and the urgency of his body against hers were the same, and she gave herself up to that timeless rhythm that was destruction and creation together, and listened for the cry that would be birth and death.

2

"GOOD MORNING." A long finger stroked her from ear to chin, and Cady yawned and flexed her muscles in the confined space. The sun was shining brightly through the orange fabric of the tent, covering everything with a rather interesting glow.

"It is, isn't it?" She touched the naked skin near her hand. Her head was on Luke's shoulder, her body stretched along the length of his, his arms around her. Cady could hardly believe they had slept so close all night long without getting into a battle for space or an uncomfortable tangle of elbows and knees.

She raised her head and looked down into Luke's sleepy face. "Did you sleep?" she asked in sudden suspicion.

"Very well, thank you," he said, grinning. "Did you?"

"Mmm," she said. She turned and lightly kicked an experimental foot. "Is this sleeping bag bigger than normal?"

"Nope. Regulation size."

She snuggled back into his shoulder. "I wonder if this is how twins feel in the womb?"

Luke laughed lazily. "In the ninth month?"

Cady took the hint; she was good at taking hints. If her years in foster homes had taught her one thing, it was to know immediately when you were not wanted, and disappear.

"Right," she agreed easily. "Time for getting out into the cold, unwelcoming world!"

Luke grunted regretfully as she slid open the zipper. "Already?" he drawled in sleepy laziness. "No more morning cuddle than that?"

She smiled at him, feeling an odd pull on her heartstrings. It was kind of him to say that: he was a big man and must be very uncomfortable with her squashed in beside him. Yet he didn't rush her or make noises of relief. He must be the kindest man she had ever known.

"Come on, lazybones!" She grinned, reaching for her jersey top, which lay in a bundle nearby, and pulling it over her head. It was damp and cold and she shivered. "Didn't you say you wanted to make an early start this morning?" If he left now she would feel lonely, she knew; she didn't want him to go. But still less did she want to appear clinging.

The hand that had been lazily stroking her dark hair paused. "Yes," said Luke in a rather odd tone. "I guess I'd better get moving. You're staying on here?"

His voice sounded just a little as though he'd been slapped, and she turned to him in sudden dismay. Oh God, had she spoiled it? Would he have wanted to stay a while?

"Did you—" she began, but he was patting her backside, saying with a grin, "Come on, woman, you're letting in a draft, sitting there like that! Let me get my clothes on!" And it was too late to recapture the mood, too late to ask him to stay. Cady was filled with regret.

She laughed and responded in kind, and they bantered good-naturedly while she slipped on the furry cream trousers, undid the tent flap and poked her head outside.

It was a beautiful fall day. Indian summer had not passed with last night's storm. Cady stood up and drank in the warmth of the sun. "It's gorgeous!" she called to Luke. "Going to be a perfect day!"

By all the signs there hadn't been much rain. Her tent

was perfectly high and dry, and the plastic she had stretched over the fire site and the wood had only the tiniest puddle of water in it. In sudden embarrassment that he should think she had panicked over a little rain, Cady pulled the green plastic out from under the small rocks she had held it down with and folded it up. In her tent she stuffed it back into her pack, pulled out toilet paper, slipped on her boots and clomped off into the bushes.

Luke was down by the lake when she returned, and when she had finished dressing and washing he was at work laying the fire. Cady filled a saucepan with water and brought it to the fire.

They worked well together, each looking out for what needed doing and doing it. Cady made tea and porridge and reconstituted some powdered milk while Luke packed his tent and most of his gear.

"Good grief!" he exclaimed, looking into the bubbling pot in pretended horror when he had finished. "What's that glop?"

"Red River Cereal," she told him serenely. "It's hot and filling and good for you."

"For breakfast?" he protested. "For human beings?"

Cady laughed and resolutely spooned some of the mixture onto his plate. "Yes, for humans," she told him. "Here, try it. It's probably just what your mother used to make."

"Not my mother," Luke assured her hastily, but he accepted the dish from her with a good grace and fell to spooning honey and milk over it. "My mother fed me good old Kellogg's Corn Flakes. She still does, when she gets the chance."

He glanced over his shoulder toward his pack and Cady, following his glance, gurgled into laughter. He had packed everything but his breakfast needs, and there, leaning against the orange backpack, was a familiar-looking box of Kellogg's Corn Flakes.

"Oh, well," she said, giggling, "I can't say you didn't grow up big and strong on it." Then she choked and blinked and was caught in the dark beam of his gaze.

Luke grinned. "You, too," he agreed. After a wicked moment his gaze set her free and he took his first spoonful of the hot cereal. He rolled his eyes a little and made a business of swallowing. "Though I gotta say, if your mother fed you this stuff she was one weird broad."

Cady laughed. One or two of them had been, she supposed, but she couldn't remember which of her many "mothers" had fed her Red River Cereal for breakfast. "Oh, well," she said, "winters are colder in Saskatchewan."

"Is that where you were raised? And what about the summers?"

Cady swallowed a mouthful of sweet, warm porridge and milk. "Nabisco Shredded Wheat," she confided.

"Oh," said Luke. "We'd better call off the wedding." He sounded crestfallen. "Intercultural marriages are so difficult."

He kept her laughing right up to the moment he left, but always in the back of her mind was the knowledge that when he did leave she would never see him again. It seemed dreadful that someone she felt so close to would soon be gone so permanently, but Cady did not know how to ask for more.

When he had loaded up his canoe and was ready to push off, he turned. "How long are you staying on this lake, Cady?"

His blue eyes were almost navy this morning, and he sounded as though it were important to him. But Cady couldn't let her guard down.

"Oh—two or three days." She shrugged.

"Make it three, will you?" he asked earnestly. "Will you promise to make it three? I need time to think. I've got— Will you stay here till Friday?"

That was three nights and three days. It would be hellish, waiting in inactivity, and what if he never came back? Cady had had lots of experience of waiting for people who never came back. She had already done a lifetime's waiting. She shrugged.

"Thursday," she said. "I'll probably leave Thursday. If I'm lazy for too long my muscles will seize up."

Luke looked at her and nodded his head. "You're sure you won't leave before?"

She smiled against the sudden rage inside her. Why was he asking her to wait? If he was so interested, why was he leaving at all? Suddenly she realized that he was just being polite, that this was his way of softening the blow.

"Look," she said. "Don't worry about me, Luke. I know what a one-night stand is. I'm okay."

His face was shuttered, and she could have kicked herself for causing it. Maybe he had meant what he'd said. Maybe he was really— "Look," she began, "I—"

"Never mind, Cady," he said gently. "I understand. It's been nice knowing you. Really nice. So long."

He pushed the canoe off and jumped agilely inside, and then with a last wave he turned and began to paddle. He was very competent in a canoe. Cady blinked hard and swallowed, and before he was even halfway across the lake, turned and walked into the woods in search of fuel.

GRADUALLY SHE FORCED HER BRAIN to abandon thoughts of Luke and return to the problem she had come to Algonquin to sort out: Miles Davidson. When she had come back to Canada a few weeks ago she hadn't even been exactly sure what her reasons were. A little homesickness, of course, and the fatigue of living in England's problem-ridden economy. No matter how hard she worked, and she had worked hard—Cady was what they called a "working actress," she might not be famous, but she could always get a job and she worked steadily—no matter how hard she worked, there was never enough money. She owned a small flat in an un-posh area of London, and for four years she had been protected from the horror of exorbitant rents, but even so, she had been lucky to be able to afford one new piece of furniture a year.

She had tired of it, as she had tired of gray winters and wet summers. And although there was no one in Canada to make the country "home" to her except a few friends in Toronto, she had decided to come home for a year's rest, to a place where life would lack both the excitement and the strain of life in London.

She had expected to find work fairly soon. She still had her Canadian accent at her command, and she had begun using it as soon as she got off the plane in Toronto. There was no point in being typecast as Lady Bracknell's niece the minute she opened her mouth.

She had expected to find work, but she had not expected to walk into an interview with the man in line to be the next "brilliant" young director from Hollywood, Miles Davidson. Nor had she expected to be considered for one of the female leads in the film he was casting.

But Miles Davidson liked her, and Canadian interests were backing some of the film, and he was supposed to cast one of the leads and two of the supporting roles with Canadian talent. For this particular part, he had narrowed his choices down to three, and Cady was one of them.

A screen test had followed, and now Miles Davidson would narrow it down even more, and perhaps one of the three would get to do a nude screen test. And that one might get the part, or Miles Davidson might have to start all over again.

Cady was on the edge of making it, on the edge of making the transition from working actress to star. It was so close she could taste it.

And then Miles Davidson had told her about the friend's cottage he had borrowed up on the French River, and how Cady would be expected to spend a weekend there with him while he coached her for the nude screen test.

She had never before in her career been faced with such a decision, though she had friends who had. She had never been up for a star part before, had never played the West End. She had worked her way up in rep, and in six years had moved from smaller parts in little reps to leads in the world-famous English repertory theaters.

This movie could catapult her to stardom. Miles Davidson had three well-known feature films in his immediate past, each progressively more successful than the last. *Love and Regret* was going to be his blockbuster. *Love and Regret* was going to kick him, and everyone else connected with it, into stardom. Either that, or it was going to bomb; and the whole film world would be watching to see which.

There were two nude scenes in the film, a commonplace these days. Cady herself was not in the least dismayed by the idea. She belonged to a generation of actors for whom nudity in the pursuit of art was expected, was taken for granted. Cady had done her growing up during the great revolution against puritanism and censorship in the theater, and by the time she was eighteen, the battle was over. When nudity contributed to art or theater, as far as Cady and most of her contemporaries were concerned, it was justified—even necessary.

For Cady, art truly was the governing factor. She would not have posed nude for *Playboy*, but she would play the hysterical breakdown scene in *Love and Regret* naked without any sense of compromise, and the almost brutally tender bedroom scene as well.

She would if she got the chance. But there was no way she would get the chance, Cady knew, if she did not do a nude screen test.

And that was the tacit promise being held out to her: if she slept with Miles Davidson she would get a nude screen test.

He could not guarantee her the part, because he didn't have complete casting authority, and the script called for the woman to have a beautiful body. Cady had a beautiful body, she knew. Probably more beautiful than Miles Davidson expected. She was very slim waisted; she had rounded hips, full high breasts and very good legs. She was one of the blessed, and she knew it. That screen test, all other things being equal, could well clinch her the part.

A weekend on the French River with a man she did not love could get her the first feature-film lead of her career. It could change her life.

Cady sat down on a fallen log and absentmindedly shredded a red maple leaf, and then another.

She had spent last night with a man she didn't love, hadn't she? Why should a weekend with Miles Davidson be any different? He wasn't old and he wasn't ugly. He wasn't even repulsive. In his thin, intense way he was interesting, even exciting. She liked the way he spoke, the way he enthused about a role, getting right inside the character's motivations. He was probably a brilliant director. She would probably work very well with him. If there was a film director who was going to get the best from her it might well be Miles Davidson.

Oh, *why* was the decision so hard to make? Why couldn't she just say yes and be done with it?

Because she wouldn't be done with it. Because she would be selling her body and, with it, a piece of her soul. How large a piece of her soul she would not know till afterward, nor how difficult it would be to get along without it.

When she had shredded all the leaves on the twig she held, Cady flung it away, bent to pick up her small collection of firewood and headed back to the campsite.

Tuesday today. Miles had been in Los Angeles for four days. He would have flown out with the three tests Saturday to show them to his American backers. One of a Canadian, one of an American and one marked "Kate Hunter." A good, English-sounding name, her London agent had said, choosing it for her, anxious that Cady not be saddled with a name that would make producers think of her as American.

She might be able to change it back now, if she got this part. If she were going to be a star, she would like to do it under her own name. If she were going to stay in North America to work, now would be the time to become Cady Hunter again.

The sun was high and warm, beating down through the trees onto her head as she bent to add twigs to the armful that would fuel her fire tonight. She couldn't have asked for a better day in which to do her laundry and bathe and wash her hair. The water would still be cold, of course, but the sunshine would warm her afterward.

She entered the campsite again with the faintest twinge of regret that it was empty. She had enjoyed talking to Luke last night. She would have liked to make and eat lunch with him and laze away the afternoon with conversation. Sometimes being alone was a pleasure, and sometimes it was as though every activity was a make-work project designed to keep loneliness at bay. Till yesterday she had enjoyed her solitude, but Luke had disturbed her peace. Now she wished she had moved on this morning, filling the solitary hours with hard work and new sights. Perhaps she would move on in the morning.

But as soon as the thought crossed her mind, she knew that she would not leave. She would stay here till Thursday, and probably till Friday, waiting for Luke to come back.

Waiting. She was always waiting. When would the waiting stop?

SHE BOILED WATER FOR TEA, but ate only a cold sandwich for lunch. She seemed to have lost her appetite again, not having spent the morning paddling. She pulled off her sweater and lay back in her T-shirt, soaking up the sun and thinking.

Thea had not been able to offer much help. Thea, whose flat Cady had shared since her return to Toronto, was a comedy-revue actress who had been working with the same popular ensemble for years. Nothing ever surprised Thea, and nothing ever shocked her, and when Cady had told her about Miles Davidson's veiled ultimatum, she had expected Thea to advise her to jump at it.

"Well, *I* could do it," Thea had said thoughtfully. "Unless he's weird or something, but I never heard that he is. And if it were anyone else, Cady, I'd probably say go ahead, you know? Just close your eyes and pretend. Or else, make yourself fall in love with him. That's how I'd do it. I'd build up such a crush on him he'd be doing me a favor. But I don't know, Cady—you're different, you know? You've got—hell, I don't know!—a kind of inner fragility, as though your sense of yourself would be easily broken. And I don't know how you'd. . . . Do you see what I'm saying?"

"I guess so," Cady said unhappily. "You think I'm too weak to—"

Thea shook her head energetically. "No," she interrupted. "Not weak, Cady. Too bruised, maybe. Too hurt. Sometimes I wonder how much of the world's pain you can take. You know, most of us had an ordinary reasonably happy childhood—when the world starts kicking us around we've got a certain resilience. But you've been kicked around all your life. Why you picked the meanest profession going I'll never know. Maybe habit. Maybe you subconsciously chose a profession that would continue the kind of life-style you were used to."

"I love acting," Cady said firmly.

"Sure you do. We all do. That doesn't change the fact that it's the most neurotic profession you can go into and still stay legal."

Cady laughed aloud at that. "So where does that leave us?" she demanded.

"With a few exceptions," Thea said firmly, "it leaves us getting our jollies on stage because we don't know how to get them in ordinary human relationships."

Well, that was certainly a sobering thought, not entirely new to Cady. Her first love in acting would always be the stage, and she knew that was because of the direct connection with the audience, the sense of power she sometimes felt over them, the love that came back at her when she had given them her best.

So Thea had had no advice for her, and Cady did not know or trust the agent who had taken her on when she had returned to Toronto well enough to discuss the problem with her.

Cady stirred and opened her eyes. She was half asleep, and the afternoon was moving on. She had lots to do before the sun went down.

She did her laundry in a pot over the fire, and strung up a clothesline for it, wishing she had washed her things out first thing this morning and given them the whole day to dry. Then she combed out her hair and stripped, and picking up her biodegradable soap and shampoo she went down to the lake to bathe.

It was icy cold. Cady soaped herself quickly all over, shampooed her hair, then dived under the surface and swam swiftly, silently through rich depths, through the shafts of filtered sunlight and the haze of all the countless microscopic beings that still were able to make this lake their home.

This lake was still healthy. Cady had seen a dying lake, a lake where rain bearing the pollution of countless industrial plants had mercilessly fallen, far from the cities, far from the industrial belt; had fallen to destroy the balance of nature in the wilderness lakes, killing off first the microscopic beings, then the plankton, and so up the long chain toward the fish.

She had seen a lake like that, a dying lake that looked glistening, clear and radiant with health. She had seen it on a television documentary in England and heard the report that her wilderness was dying in her absence, that hundreds, thousands of Canadian lakes were dying every year. She had sat in stunned disbelief; and was it then that her vague plans for a visit home had crystalized into determination?

She stayed in the living water as long as she could, accepting the cold, making it part of her, till she was no longer sure where her body left off and the lake began. This could be the last time. By next summer this lake, too, might be dead. Cady was conscious of the fact that this trip was less to reestablish contact with the heart of her country than to make a prolonged goodbye to the fortress of undisturbed wilderness that she loved so much. A fortress whose walls were crumbling under the killing blows of the soft, steady fall of raindrops.

THAT NIGHT WAS LONELIER than anything she had experienced for years. Cady built the fire up so that it burned brightly against the night, but somehow its comforting glow only increased her sense of isolation. She was cut

off from the world; she had always been cut off, but
somehow she had learned to enjoy her isolation, calling
it independence.

How many days and nights, she wondered, had she
kept herself from loneliness by telling herself she enjoyed solitude? She wasn't enjoying it tonight. The con-
trast with last night was too great—that long, lazy talk
by the fire while the time had flown.

Tonight the time passed slowly. Between sunset and
moonrise was an age. Cady sat on a stone and stared
into the flames, her uneaten dinner cold on the plate.
She was almost desolate, as desolate as she had been on
those other, long-ago nights when she had sat and waited for someone who would never come back.

Then she had not believed; she had refused to accept
what she had been told, and even now the child part of
her was saying over and over inside her, *he will come
back, he will, he will, he will.*

She knew he would not come back. She knew, even,
that she had driven him away, and the child inside her
recognized the knowledge. *Why won't they come back?*
She heard her own childish voice down through the long
years, and tonight the memory was too sharp, too close,
and she felt tears burn her eyelids. *Don't they love me
anymore? Is it because I was bad? But I won't be bad
anymore! Tell them I promise to be good!*

Cady squeezed her eyes shut and fought back the
memory. What was the point in letting yourself remember? You had to close the door on the past and go on. It
was odd that she should be remembering all that stuff
now. Was it Luke who had dredged it all up, his absence
making her feel so alone?

Suddenly she took her eyes from the fire and flicked a
glance at the dark forest around her. She shivered.
Maybe it was just the environment. She'd been stupid to
come here all alone for so long, where if the walls of the

forest closed in on you there would be no human contact, no way to save yourself. She had never been frightened of the forest before, but now the darkness seemed violently threatening.

"Get a grip on yourself," Cady muttered out loud, and stood up and methodically began to prepare the campsite for the night.

She would start back tomorrow, she told herself calmly. She would start right after breakfast—she glanced at the clothesline hung with her washing—or as soon as her clothes were dry. Even so, the trip out would take four days—three if she pushed it. Cady cursed herself. She should have had more sense than to come so deep into the bush on her first trip in six years. She should have done a zigzag pattern so that she was never more than a day's journey out.

Well, it was too late for regrets. She would make it back. She always made it, though she might not enjoy the trip much.

As she moved around the campsite in ordinary activity, checking the fire, stowing her food for the night and getting ready for bed, her fear subsided. Things would seem better in the morning. Cady slid into her sleeping bag and settled for sleep. She wasn't really afraid to be alone. She liked it. It was just that Luke had reminded her of the bad times, that was all. And she hated to remember the bad times.

SWEAT POURED OFF Luke's face and body far in excess of what the heat of the day and the exertion of paddling demanded, so that every square inch of his T-shirt was plastered to his skin dripping wet, and he was half blinded by the drops of water falling into his eyes. He paddled the canoe clumsily, blindly, stopping only when the pain became unbearable, to dip his arm for a moment into the soothing touch of the lake water. The sun seemed unseasonably hot to him. He was grateful that the water did not, for without its cold periodically numbing the pain, he must certainly have given up long ago. Even as it was, he knew he was at the end of his endurance. If he didn't find the campsite soon....

There it was, the green tent in the same position as when he had left. He could not see Cady, but the smoke drifting up from her fire and the presence of the silver canoe meant that she was in the camp. Just as Luke was deciding that he was getting close enough to shout, there was a disturbance in the water about thirty feet ahead of him, and through the film of perspiration over his eyes he saw her burst out of the water and head up the beach to her tent.

Well, she had seen him. Good. No need to shout. The current had been with him since the middle of the lake, and when he saw that it would carry him directly to the beach he let himself stop paddling; the wind and the current kindly beached him on the short strip of sand.

"It *is* you," she said in surprise, and he looked up to see her standing at the bow, dressed now in jeans and a shirt, her hair in a towel, her blue eyes narrowing as she jerked to look more closely. He thought dimly how much he liked her eyes.

"What's wrong?" she asked in her husky voice. "I thought you were somebody drunk, somebody who didn't know how to—" She stopped as he held up his left arm and tried to remember how to speak. "Oh, my gosh," Cady exclaimed, splashing down into the water by his side. She took the paddle from him and dropped it into the canoe. "Come on," she urged, pulling his right arm over her shoulder. "Come on, get out."

Somehow he did so without the canoe capsizing, and as she half carried him up the beach he struggled to find his voice. She led him up to sit by the fire, and when he felt the ground under him he smiled up at her.

"I guess you can't keep me away," Luke said, and fainted.

3

"AWAKE?" CADY ASKED SOFTLY. He had begun to get restless, and she eyed him in concern. She wished he would wake up. Other than the evidence before her eyes—that his arm was covered with about a million blisters—she had no idea what was wrong with him. Had he fallen, hit his head? Was he sick?

She was virtually without medicine, except for her vitamins and a tiny first-aid kit. The best she had been able to do was dig a small trough for his arm, line it as well as she could with a plastic garbage bag and keep it filled with water. She had been moving back and forth between Luke and the lake with the large saucepan all afternoon. The water kept slowly draining away in spite of the plastic lining; in any case she knew the constant renewal of its icy coldness would help to reduce the shock to his burned skin.

It was obvious he had burned himself somehow, but what else had he done? She wished he would wake up. It was nearly sunset.

"Awake?" she asked again when he stirred, and this time she was rewarded with a sleepy murmur.

"Mmm?" inquired Luke, and his dark eyebrows closed above his nose in a frown of pain. "Cady?" and then a large sigh and a satisfied "Cady." The frown lifted and he opened his blue eyes and smiled up at her. Her heart was inexpressibly lightened.

"How do you feel?"

"How do I—" he began curiously, making a movement to sit up. The question changed to a grunt of pain as he bent the blistered elbow of his left arm. "Yow!" he whispered in surprise, lying back. "What the hell has happened?"

"That's what I'm waiting to hear," Cady told him. "Wait a sec." She picked up the saucepan and made another trip to the lake. His grimace of pain relaxed as she poured the water gently over his arm.

"That's better," he said gratefully, shutting his eyes. "I burned myself, didn't I?"

"Looks like it," agreed Cady, a sigh of relief betraying her fear that he was so sick he wouldn't remember. "How?"

"How is the question, all right," Luke said in some disgust. He shook his head then, and became aware that he was cocooned in a sleeping bag. Lifting his head to look he demanded, "Is this your sleeping bag? Where's mine?"

"You came without your pack, I'm afraid. And I didn't know where to begin looking for it. Anyway, I didn't want to leave you—I wasn't sure what was wrong."

"Hmm." Luke eyed the position of the sun. "I set up camp down the river, just short of the next portage. Too late to go get it now, but it'll be all right till morning. I managed to put the fire out."

Cady wrinkled her brow in surprise. "You camped before the next portage?" she repeated. If she'd known that, she might have risked leaving him here for the couple of hours it would take to go and retrieve his gear. She couldn't go now; she couldn't risk canoeing into unknown waters after dark. "But why—"

He interrupted. "I'm not sure quite how this happened. I was boiling water for lunch . . . I guess I left the handle on the pot too long. When I picked it up it burned my damn hand, and trying to keep the water clear of the fire I spilled it all over my arm instead." He chuckled faintly, then winced as he involuntarily bent his arm again. "I let out a bellow like a moose," he told her with a grin. "Is it mating season for mooses? I was afraid it was. I kept expecting a voracious lady moose to charge out of the woods and challenge me to make good on my promise."

Cady laughed helplessly. "You're delirious," she told him.

"Yes, but *is* it mating season for mooses?" Luke pressed mock-worriedly.

"If it is," Cady gurgled, "your lady moose will probably tear up the campsite in righteous fury. Yours, I hope," she added. "If she tracks you down here we're in for it."

"That's my luck, is it?" Luke asked ruefully. "Tracked across the wilderness by a moose, but the lady I hoped would be on my trail wasn't nearly so determined."

She blinked and gasped and her stomach did a curious flip-flop; and all the time Luke's blue eyes were gazing straight into hers so that she could not hide her reactions from him.

Cady turned and reached for the bottle on the ground beside her. "Here," she said huskily. "Can you sit up enough to swallow?" She opened the bottle and slid a dozen oblong tablets onto her palm.

"So many?" asked Luke in surprise, propping himself up on his good right arm. "What are they?"

"Vitamin C," Cady told him, popping one into his mouth and holding the cup of water to his lips. Luke drank and swallowed, and she popped in another. "To fight infection."

His hair was thick and silky under her fingers as she held his head unnecessarily while he drank. Ten times she put her fingers into his mouth, and ten times his soft, sensuous lips brushed her sensitive fingertips as he took the vitamin tablet from her.

"No antibiotics?" he asked teasingly after number five, and she smiled down at him. Somehow she had drawn closer and closer to him so that now she supported his head against her breast as she lifted the cup to his mouth.

The caress of his mouth reminded her of the night before last and the other places where his lips had touched and teased her. His head lay on her breast as a child's might, his lips close to the nipple hidden under the soft cloth, but it was not as a child she saw him, and it was not for a child's mouth that her breast ached with need.

When the last tablet was gone and her palm was empty Luke lay back, and just for a moment she hovered above him. His breathing was ragged, and before she could move to break the spell that enveloped them his fingers closed on her arm.

"Cady," he said softly, looking straight into her eyes, and she bent her head as he lifted his.

The kiss pierced her to the womb with a sweetness that melted her bones, and she closed her eyes and smiled as he kissed her, and lifted her head again.

"We have a problem," she informed him softly.

"Still?" Luke asked ruefully, lowering his head reluctantly to the ground again.

Cady missed the innuendo. "We have two people, and only one sleeping bag," she informed him gravely.

Luke raised his eyebrows. "There were two of us the other night, too," he pointed out.

"But one of us was not a walking wounded."

"Oh!" returned Luke. He glanced at his arm. "Are you trying to tell me you're averse to keeping close quarters with a wound?"

"What?" she demanded. "No, Luke, it's you! You'll be uncomfortable enough as it is, without having to share a sleeping bag. I was wondering if you think I could make it up to your campsite and back before it gets too dark to navigate properly."

Obediently he eyed the sun, then shook his head. "I don't, Cady," he said apologetically. "Not really. If you really *have* to sleep alone tonight, I've got a flashlight—Oh, no I don't, it's at the site. Have you got a flashlight?"

"A small one." She did not relish the thought of a canoe trip after dark, searching for a campsite that she had never seen before. Especially not with a wounded Luke along, which she knew he was going to suggest. Her voice reflected her doubts.

"Look," said Luke, "I'll be all right. I certainly won't be any less comfortable because you're sleeping with me. *You* might be if I get restless, but I promise you this arm hurts enough that *I* won't. I won't even notice if you get me with a toenail."

That made her laugh. She stood up and dusted her hands on her jeans, then routinely checked her hair to see if it had dried.

"I'll have to dry this by the fire," she said. "Or we'll both end up with a cold tomorrow." Today she had meant to swim without getting her hair wet, because her hair was thick, the nights were cold and she had washed her hair yesterday. But once in the water she hadn't been able to resist the lure of the rich, dark depths. "In the meantime, what would you like for supper?"

There was a bubble of laughter in her voice, and she knew she was happy because Luke had come back and tonight would not be lonely, as last night had been. "Think about it while I get some water for your arm," she told him.

Cady picked up the saucepan and ran lightly down to the water's edge. There she stood still for a moment, breathing in the fresh evening air, the scents and sounds of the wilderness, with a pleasure that was heightened because it could be shared. That experience was new and strange to her, and she turned it over wonderingly in her mind.

Behind her Luke lay with his head turned to one side, watching the tall, straight figure that faced the sun so joyfully. She had an electric vitality he had never met in a woman before. "Like a creature of another race," he mused aloud. "Another planet, say. A perfect human, fulfilling the potential that we all have.... 'Dark are they, and long of limb, with a beauty that is wild and free....' Have I heard that somewhere before? An entire race of Cadys, and the inhabitants of Earth will be envious and full of fear and want to kill them, except for a few who will love them and learn from them and end up themselves perfected humans...."

He was startled into awareness by cold water falling over his arm and her rich, clear voice saying, "You're muttering to yourself. Are you delirious again? Or are you deciding what you want?" And Luke looked up and smiled at his own thoughts.

"I've already decided," he said softly.

"Well?"

She was talking about supper. "Steak, tomatoes, beans and a baked potato," Luke rattled off with a grin.

Cady grinned back. "What, no processed cheese slices, no packaged TV dinner full of delicious chemicals, dyes and additives?"

His grin broadened as though he had her now. "Oh, I don't expect a *civilized* meal here in the wilderness!"

"Love fifteen," Cady acknowledged, and he laughed outright.

She made rice and meat into a modified beef Stroganoff, and peas. She left her own food near the fire to keep warm and spoon-fed Luke, whose arm was too painful to be kept out of the cold water for the awkward business of sitting up and eating one-handed. But neither of them wanted to ask whether the real reason was simply that they drew pleasure from the closeness.

Later Cady built up the fire and brushed her long hair

in its warm flickering glow, aware that Luke watched her, aware that to him the sight was a sensual pleasure.

She had put a numbing ointment on his arm, and some of her small hoard of aloe-vera gel, and although he still dipped it in cold water from time to time, he could sit up and was looking a little more comfortable.

He said, "So what was it like, growing up on the prairies? What town did you grow up in, in Saskatchewan?"

"Just about all of them, I sometimes think," she returned with a grin.

Luke looked momentarily puzzled. "What were you, an army brat?"

"No, I was a difficult foster child. No one could stand me longer than a few months."

It was out so easily, though she didn't talk about it often, and never to men. Never once to a lover. Perhaps there was a first time for everything.

"I see." Luke's voice was quiet, and he sounded as though he really did see. "Where were your parents?"

"They died," she replied, her voice bright with a defense against the pain that ought to have been muted long ago, but somehow never had.

"I'm sorry," said Luke. "That must have hurt you."

"I didn't want them to go out that day," she recalled, feeling the bitterness well up inside, the bitterness she hadn't been able to put to rest in twenty-five long years. "I screamed, I threw a tantrum, though I'm sure normally I didn't do that—I have vague memories of having baby-sitters before that, and no memory of making a fuss like that." Cady breathed deeply. She wanted to stop, she didn't want to tell him this, but a part of her was trembling with the need to tell him. She reached out to throw another log on the fire. "That's odd, isn't it? I always think it was strange, my not wanting them to go. I don't know where they were going—it must have been just an afternoon thing, because they promised they'd be home before I went to bed. But they didn't come, and it was past my bedtime, and the baby-sitter tried to get me to go to bed. I was hysterical, I didn't want to go, they'd promised me, but finally I guess I fell asleep out of sheer exhaustion.

"I woke up later, when there were voices downstairs. My grandparents were there, and my grandmother was crying and so was the baby-sitter. My parents had left me. They were never coming back, no matter how much I wanted them to."

"What was it?" Luke asked.

"Oh, a car accident. Two teenagers out joyriding, it said in the papers. I looked it up later, when I was old enough."

"How old were you when it happened?"

"Two and a half. I know people don't remember things that early, but I remember it. I remember every second as though it were a year. It's amazing what can go on in one second. How much the human mind can learn in one little second."

In the silence the fire spat, and Luke shifted to lower his arm into the trench of water. Cady came to with a start.

"Well, how boring!" she said with a little laugh.

Luke straightened up again and looked into her eyes in the firelight. "I'm not bored. I'm interested. Is that when the foster homes started?"

She said, "Why don't you tell me what it's like to grow up in a nice, ordinary family where your mother fed you cornflakes for breakfast?" and there was more than curiosity in her tone; there was a deep thread of longing that he knew she couldn't hear herself.

"Because that won't take my mind off my arm," he said. "You do. Tell me about the foster homes."

"Oh, I didn't get fostered out then. That was later.

First my grandparents took me to live with them, in a small town called Sturgis. I stayed with them till I was nearly six."

She stopped and absently stirred the fire with a stick.

"Till you were six?" Luke prompted.

Suddenly she was nearly crying. She couldn't believe it. *Crying* over such ancient history! Cady stood up with the saucepan. "You must need a refill," she told him, and headed down to the lake in the darkness.

He was silent when she returned, letting her pour the water over his painful burns and then thanking her softly. She returned to her seat by the fire, and he let her spend a minute in reverie, then queried softly, "What happened when you were six?"

"The same thing," she replied quietly, from her abstraction. She was a long way away, looking down a road he had never traveled, into a deep pain he could only learn about secondhand. "Exactly the same thing. They went away, and I had a baby-sitter, one of the women from church. I didn't want to go to bed, but I did, and then she was waking me up, and she was crying, and I knew I didn't have anybody in the world, and I never would have again. The next day they came and got me. They moved me to another town and another school—and I never said goodbye. Not to anyone in Sturgis, not even my best friend Shirley."

He was almost too horrified to speak. "It's a wonder you didn't go mad," he said.

"Oh, I'm sure I did!" Cady laughed a tinkling laugh. "There are different ways of going crazy. I wouldn't go to bed at night, and when I did I used to wake up screaming. I don't know why. I don't remember the dream. I'd wake up screaming, and I wouldn't be able to stop. At one place they threw a bucket of water in my face. The next day I was moved—another family, another school."

"Did you have time to say goodbye that time?"

Cady shrugged. "Oh, by then I didn't care about saying goodbye. It didn't matter. Nobody cared. You don't make friends when you're only in a place two or three months. Or two weeks."

"No, I guess not."

Cady stood up and dusted off her jeans, a dismissive gesture he recognized. "I was a sentimental kid, that was my problem. But I grew out of it, thank God. I don't need to say goodbye anymore—there are always new places, new people to meet."

She looked at him steadily in the darkness, as though sending him some message she herself was hardly aware of. She had almost forgotten that early sense of knowing him, of knowing that he would be safe. If Cady's life had taught her one thing, it was that nothing in life was safe.

She walked to her tent to pick up the small first-aid kit she had brought with her, and when she returned Luke was gazing at his blistered left arm with a thoughtful half-smile on his face.

Gently she spread more ointment over the burn, then dipped a cylinder of white bandage in the water and set out to wrap his arm.

"This'll stay wet for a while," she pointed out. "You can pour a little water on it during the night and maybe it'll keep cold long enough for you to get some sleep."

"I'm sure I will," he agreed easily, though the only painkillers she had to offer were aspirin, and he was lucky to get those. She didn't take painkillers as a rule and had only brought them along on this trip as an afterthought.

Tonight Cady prepared the campsite for the night alone, seeing to the food and fire and moving the sleeping bag back into the tent. They took turns in the tent undressing, which seemed odd considering the intimacy

of their first night and the fact that they would be sharing the same sleeping bag. But Luke seemed to sense her
need for privacy and raised no query. Cady in any case
was quick; she was in the tent only for a minute or two
before coming out in her track suit, carrying her tooth-
brush and towel down to the water's edge.

It was odd, this sudden need to put distance between
them. She had felt so close to him before...before this
evening. Before she had told him about her past? Her
mouth full of toothpaste, Cady snorted in amusement.
That was it, of course. She had never been the kind to
open her heart to people. Probably the only person in
the world who knew as much as she had told Luke
about herself was Thea. And perhaps that long-ago foster mother who had listened and cared.

No wonder she felt awkward and ill at ease now! Telling a total stranger everything there was to know about
herself! It had taken her years to tell Thea as much.

He was settled into the sleeping bag by the time she
got back to the tent, a saucepan of water within arm's
reach, the tent's interior lighted by the small warm glow
of the candle she had read by last night. He was lazily
flipping through her book, which rested against his
knees, with his good hand. His dark hair was tousled
and the black hair of his chest and arms and the growth
of his beard seemed very masculine in the small space.

But his face looked more relaxed than it had all day,
and she thought the aspirins must be working finally,
for the grim look of constant pain was eased.

He put down the book as she knelt down to stow her
things in her pack. "Good read?" he asked curiously,
and she shrugged in embarrassment; the book was a
love story.

"Actually, it is," she began defensively. "It's very well
written. Books like that are great for taking your mind
off things, and I've got a lot on my mind at the...."

Luke looked at her. "Don't apologize to me," he said with a grin. "I like escape fiction myself—a different variety, of course. It all gets sneered at, one way or another, at some time in history."

"Yeah?" she asked with a disbelieving smile. "I've never heard detective fiction get slammed the way romance does."

He had the grace to chuckle. "Well, perhaps not. But then, women's tastes and attitudes come in for a certain amount of contempt anyway, don't they?"

"Do they?"

Luke mused, "I once heard my father say to my mother after a small dinner party, 'I suppose the women were talking about babies again.' He said it in a tone of such tolerant contempt I was amazed my mother didn't react. They both took it for granted that his conversation with the men had been significant and intellectual. Yet I had spent the evening with the men, and what they had talked about was cars, football and politics. Far less significant, when you look at it, than children and babies."

"Aren't they about the same?" Cady protested mildly, wondering if this conversation was designed to ease whatever mild embarrassment she might feel as she crawled in beside him and fitted her long legs into the space left by his.

"Do you think so? I think the human is more significant than the mechanical. And women are traditionally more in touch with the human than men. I'd say, 'by nature,' except that you might be a raving feminist and shout 'biology is not destiny' at me." He smiled questioningly at her.

Cady shrugged as well as she could in the cramped space. "Oh, well," she said, "for some people biology is destiny, and for some it isn't. I haven't any argument with either type, as long as they leave me alone."

"Leave you alone?"

"As long as the traditionalists don't nag me for not getting married and having babies and the feminists don't nag me for reading love stories. I just want to live my own life."

Luke picked up the book and looked at the cover art, a painting of a man and woman in passionate embrace. "Don't all the men and women in these books end up getting married and having babies?" he asked curiously.

"Yes, of course."

"But that's not one of your own aims?" he pursued.

"No. What difference does that make to what I read? Do Sherlock Holmes's readers all want to own a violin, a deerstalker and a magnifying glass? I wish the—"

"No, it doesn't make any difference," he agreed easily. "I'm not attacking, I'm just curious about the trends of various kinds of fiction."

"Really?" she said faintly. "Why?"

He looked momentarily surprised. "I write it," he said. "And I like—"

"You *write* romantic fiction?" she squeaked in amazement, getting up on one elbow to look down at him. "What name do you write under?"

He made as if to lift his left hand, then winced and left it where it was. "Did I say that?" He grinned. "No, I write science fiction—another much-maligned genre."

"Really? You do? It is?" Cady babbled in her surprise, and they both laughed aloud.

"Which shall I answer first?" Luke asked her.

"Just tell me all about it," she commanded, and settled down in the curve of his good arm like a child waiting for a bedtime story. "It's very exciting, knowing a writer. Do you write short stories or novels?"

"Mostly novels, these days. Some novelettes. Now and then a short story, if it's commissioned."

"When was the last time that happened?"

"A couple of years ago. *Playboy* magazine had an—"

"*Playboy* magazine? Was that—I mean, *the Playboy*?"

"You bet. They had an idea of running a sci-fi a month for a year, by twelve names. I wrote them the story but they never used it. The idea was killed after the first one or two, I forget why."

She stroked his chest absently. "So you're a 'name'?"

"Oh, fair to middling."

"I used to read science fiction when I was a teenager," she told him. "What name do you write under?"

"My own. Luke Southam."

"Goodness," she said. "Any relation?" Southam Press was one of the largest newspaper chains across Canada, so it was natural that being a writer, he would be related.

But Luke shook his head. "Not even a poor one."

Cady looked guilty. "I've never heard of you," she confessed. "I'm sure I've never read anything by you, but I used to read a lot of—"

He said easily, "If you quit ten years ago I'm not surprised. My first book of short stories was published eight years ago."

"Oh! What was the title?"

"*The Man Who Saved Time in a Bottle.*"

Cady gurgled with delighted laughter. "Just the title alone makes me sorry I quit before I got to you."

"Thank you," Luke said, mock-gravely. "Are you settled in now? Shall I blow out the candle?"

She smiled, comfortable in the curve of his arm. "Can I pour a little light relief over your arm before you do?"

"If you would, please."

She sat up and looked at him. For someone so open, he had to be pretty stoic when it came to pain. In her experience burns were the worst kind of agony going. Cady picked up the cup resting in the saucepan of water and trailed a line of cold water all along his arm, where it was absorbed by the bandage.

"Ahhh," said Luke. "That feels better." But there was the sound of laughter in his voice, and she couldn't be entirely sure he wasn't referring to the fact that her breasts rested on his chest as she leaned over him.

"You men are all alike!" she accused in a high horrified voice she had once used onstage to portray a comic spinster. "Sex will take your mind off everything!"

Since she blew out the candle immediately afterward, it had the effect of a direct invitation, and Luke laughed in the darkness. "It would if I could," he agreed. As she settled back into a comfortable position beside him she felt the lightest of kisses brush her forehead. "Thanks for taking such good care of me, Cady," he said gently.

His voice tugged at her emotions, calling up a more tender response than she wanted to give him. "S'all right," she returned sleepily. "I'm a frustrated nurse. Night, Luke."

Silence. Then, "Ever asked yourself what it is you're afraid of, Cady?"

If she had been as sleepy as she was pretending, that would still have snapped her wide awake. "Sorry?" she asked in high surprise, her English accent and choice of vocabulary coming back unbidden and sounding distinctly unnatural.

He said, "Every time we get mentally close I feel you pull back inside to some place where you feel protected. Did you ever ask yourself why you do that?"

She felt indignant and unfairly criticized. "Come on, Luke!" she protested. "You're almost a total stranger!"

"Am I? Is that how you feel about me?"

"Yes, and you know it! I met you three days ago and you were gone for one and a half of them, so I've known you exactly one-and-a-half days! If you expect me to let it all hang out after one-and-a-half days, you're—"

He interrupted. "We made love after only a few hours. You didn't mind being physically intimate, but you're afraid of being mentally intimate."

She gasped, because somewhere that hurt. "Oh, come on, Luke! I told you I know what a one-night stand is!"

"Yes, you did. There are lots of people, women especially, who get mentally intimate even for a one-night stand. Even a one-night stand can develop into something more if you let it. But this isn't a one-night stand, Cady. It never was, and we both know it. And that's what you're scared of."

She was frighteningly close to tears, the tears that always came when someone was too gentle with her, when someone cared too much. Cady had equipped herself to deal with a cold, hard world; the more cruel the world, the more efficient she became at coping. Kindness had a way of slipping in under her guard, and wounding her more deeply than anything else could.

"Why, Cady?" Luke's voice broke into her thoughts as surely as if he were reading them. "Ask yourself why."

Or was there another reason for the tears? Was it Luke saying "it was never a one-night stand" that lowered her defenses?

She could care about Luke, if she let herself. He was a man she could love, if love weren't such a dangerous occupation in the world. That made him more of a threat to her peace of mind than anyone else in the world. There was nowhere she called home, nothing in the world that held her. The only way to survive was to make sure the world never got a grip on her, she knew that. She had always known that. She must be careful not to let Luke get that painful hold on her that meant losing him would hurt.

She said, "I should have warned you, Luke. I'm not the forever kind. I've got my career, and that's my life.

I don't need anything else. I don't want anything else."

Luke took a deep, slow breath and grunted. "Well, well," he said in a tone of surprised acceptance. "Here it is at last. I've got my mission in life."

IF LUKE'S MISSION IN LIFE was to lower her guard against love, as Cady sometimes thought but was afraid to ask, in the next few days he devoted himself to it with the care and precision of a novitiate into holy orders. He worked on gaining her trust as he might have an animal's—achieving a mental closeness by slow degrees, remaining in the same position for long periods before again inching forward, until at last he was in an area of her mind that no one had inhabited before, and she felt the first stirrings of real trust and allowed him to stay.

He never said he loved her, but she read it in the gentleness of his eyes as he looked at her. Nor did she say that she loved him, but, with fear and trepidation, she knew that she did. It was something to do with the wilderness, she felt, with their distance from the real world. Here she could trust and love, with none of the threats or pressures of the world to drive her back into the safety of self-sufficiency and isolation. She allowed herself to forget what the future might hold.

She told him about the foster homes, of the constant changes, of a childhood virtually without friendship. She told him about having no place, no rights, about always coming behind the "real" children of the family.

And Luke told her about his normal, comfortable childhood, about being cherished and cared for, about Kellogg's Corn Flakes in the morning and, inevitably, the fights with his brothers at night. He had two brothers and a sister, and was an uncle several times over.

She laughed, and cried, and because of the easy way

he spoke— "You'll like Hank," he would say casually— felt the first stirrings of a sense of belonging.

It reminded her of the Good Time, as she thought of it to herself—the foster home that she had stayed in for three magic years, from the age of eleven. The foster mother who had cared about her, who had fed her Red River Cereal in the winter and Nabisco Shredded Wheat in the summer. Who had supervised her transition into womanhood with a blend of love and common sense that she could still draw strength from, even now.

"And why did you leave them?" Luke asked.

"He was transferred out of the province," she told him. "They had to move all the way to B.C. First they thought he would have the choice of Prince Albert, and I might, I just might have been able to go with them. But out of the province was another government jurisdiction. Of course I wasn't allowed to go."

"Do you visit them much?"

Cady was surprised. "No, I've never visited them. I've never seen them since they left."

"But you write to her?"

"No—no, I never did, actually."

"Why not?" His voice was softly curious in the darkness. They were sleeping in different sleeping bags but in the same tent, as they had done every night since she had paddled upriver to dismantle Luke's campsite—she didn't really know why. At first Luke had seemed more comfortable if she was near; now she didn't question the joy she got from sharing the long late-night conversations with him as all but the owls slept. It never occurred to her that he was deliberately teaching her the joys of mental intimacy, of sharing. If sometimes the thought flickered across her mind that this was what sisters and brothers must have, she never guessed that it was what he meant her to feel.

Cady shifted uncomfortably now in the warmth of

her sleeping bag, searching for the answer to his question. "I don't know, really. I— She wrote me once or twice. I wanted to write but—well, anyway, she wouldn't really care whether I wrote or not. I was just a foster kid, you know."

"People are capable of being hurt even by foster kids," Luke pointed out.

Cady couldn't help laughing. "Me hurt her?" she asked disbelievingly. "Come on, Luke, what would she care about me? She had a family, she was probably glad to get rid of me."

"She wrote you twice. By what you tell me, she cared a lot about you. When people are rejected by people they care about, they get hurt."

She was suddenly silent inside, listening. She had felt so invisible all through her childhood. Never in her life had she really believed that anyone could care enough about her that she would have the power to hurt them. Yet if she looked at it objectively . . . .

"I guess anyone would be hurt if they wrote three times—it was three letters—and never got an answer."

"I guess they would," he agreed.

She felt an odd, stabbing pain in the region of her heart, as sharp as if she were being cut with a knife. The hurt she had caused Margery Simpson somehow reached her more deeply than any memory of her own hurt. Suddenly she was breathing jerkily in the darkness, as though she brushed across tears that were too deep to reach. Luke's hand stroked her head, and then the tears were too close to fight down. As they burned hot on her cheeks Cady understood dimly that what was happening to her was being caused by Luke deliberately, that it was some sort of process. But the knowledge was too distant to touch her.

The process went on through the hot Indian-summer days and cold autumn nights that followed. There was

little to do save talk, eat and swim, for Luke's arm
would not allow him to hike, paddle or portage, and the
question of her leaving him never arose.

Sometimes it seemed to her that they might spend the
rest of their lives here, in their own magic world. She
did not think of the approaching end of the two weeks
she had given herself. She would not let herself think of
it. Somehow she knew that at the end of the two weeks
it would all be over, that Luke was a dream she must
awaken from. She knew it and accepted it, but she
didn't have to think of it. As long as the world kept
away, she could keep up the pretence.

The world did not keep away as long as scheduled.
They had planned to set out on Friday morning, and
take it as fast or as slowly as Luke's arm would allow. It
was healing nicely, but it was not ready for the hard
exertion of paddling and portaging, no matter how
much Luke insisted otherwise. They had both told the
park warden that they would be coming out on Sunday.
If they didn't do so, someone would be put to a lot of
trouble and worry.

Luke had wanted to plan on leaving Thursday, but
Cady had balked and tried to hold out for Saturday, to
give his arm more time; or to convince Luke that she
should go out alone on Thursday and send help back to
him. He had laughed at that—it was his left arm and he
was no invalid. They had compromised on Friday, and
Cady tried not to think how quickly Friday would be
here.

It came even more quickly than she expected. On
Wednesday morning she awoke, as usual, to the sound
of the tent zipper opening as Luke went out for his
morning ablutions. Cady rolled over and stretched
sleepily, then was jerked awake by the sound of Luke's,
"What in the hell—"

There was a small muttered curse and then a clank of

metal against stone, and then a long, protesting, "Oh
noooo!" that had Cady out of the sleeping bag and out
of the tent in three seconds flat, ready for any disaster.

Then she stood blinking in the early sun, gazing
stupidly across the campsite to Luke.

He was kneeling near their fire site, by the green
bag that held their provisions and which last night, as
every night, they had strung up to hang from the branch
of the handsome red-and-orange maple that overshad-
owed the campsite. She thought at first it must have
fallen down, till she saw the litter of forks, plates and
bits of food and paper that were trailed around it. A
wild animal had got to it—not, she devoutly hoped, a
bear.

"Noooo!" Luke repeated mournfully, protestingly,
and she looked at him again. He was clutching the rem-
nants of the Kellogg's Corn Flakes box with one hand,
poking desperately inside it with the other. Cady's
stunned shock turned to laughter.

"Gone!" moaned Luke, pulling the inside wrapper
futilely from the torn box and shaking and stroking it as
though to make it yield up even one tiny flake. "All
gone!" He let the paper flutter to the ground and turned
his attention to the box, which he upended with a hope
as desperate as a starving child's. As Cady moved across
to him something else caught his eye, and he dropped
the cornflakes box and reached for it.

"My bread, *too!*" he called, with a roar that made her
jump. "What! All my little cornflakes and my bread in
one fell swoop?"

The stage had certainly missed out when Luke decided to be a writer, Cady thought, laughing more helplessly than ever. There weren't many men around who
could paraphrase Shakespeare like that, for a start. He
held up two dirty bits of white bread that were all that
was left of the loaf he had been so carefully husbanding

to make it last till Sunday. "Curse you, Red Baron!" Luke shouted at the sky.

Cady shook her head helplessly. "A ham," she told him. "That's what you are, a ham."

"Easy for you to say!" he responded, picking up the green bag and rooting further in it. "Your seedy gruel glop is still intact!" He pulled out the bag of Red River Cereal and waved it at her. "Even a raccoon won't be caught dead with it, even in the middle of the night!"

There were traces of raccoon everywhere, which at least was better than bears. Small delicate claw marks were evident in the tears in the plastic and in the dirt of the campsite.

"Which shows what level *you*'re on," Cady countered, laughing. Luke, on his knees, still pawing disconsolately through the debris for traces of his favorite foods, was a sight not to be missed. "Humans are supposed to be more intelligent than raccoons," she said.

"You're right." Luke reached for the rope and pulled it hand over hand till he got to the end, which he held up for inspection. "Look at that," he commanded. "Did that knot self-destruct, or did the little beggars untie it?"

"Raccoons?" she repeated in surprise. "Untie a knot?"

"You see? You don't know; you've always thought raccoons are stupid creatures! But—" he waggled his eyebrows at her "—they are in fact very devious thinkers, particularly when it comes to manual dexterity! I have known raccoons . . . ."

Cady began to laugh and shake her head again. He was mad, completely mad. No one had ever made her laugh so ridiculously in all her life. She said, "Are you *sure* that knot didn't come undone by itself?"

Luke looked offended. "It's obvious you've never done any research on the matter. Have you ever, for example, read the treatise called 'The Raccoon Conspiracy'?"

She looked at him out of the corner of her eye. "I've never heard of it," she said. "Who wrote it?"

"I did, of course. You should read it."

He got to his feet and dusted his knees. While they were talking he had made a quick inventory of what was left. "Well, we're not too badly off," he said. "We've still got about half our provisions."

"You wrote a book called 'The Raccoon Conspiracy'? What's it about?"

"A short story. Just what the title says. We'll have to leave sooner than we planned, Cady. Today preferably, tomorrow at the latest," he said, and all the breath left her body, because suddenly the end was right there in front of her.

"Tomorrow," she said, before she could stop herself, though she knew she should know better. "Let's not go till tomorrow, Luke."

He smiled down at her, as though he understood. "All right," he said. "Tomorrow." And she was as sure as she had ever been of anything that Luke was as grateful as she for that twenty-four-hour reprieve.

THAT NIGHT they zipped the sleeping bags together and made love again, the most gentle, loving love she had ever known. This time she did not weep, but she felt as though Luke's lovemaking had touched the deepest reaches of her soul, and that she had shown him her entire self. It was the most deeply moving experience of her life. *I love you*, she thought afterward, as she snuggled against his side, but she did not say it aloud.

It was then, in the drowsy state between fulfillment and sleep, that she made her decision about Miles Davidson. Lovemaking was not just a physical act that she could suffer or engage in as a casual payment for something she wanted. Being with Luke had shown her again what she might always have known: that lovemaking was an act of mind and body and spirit all together. And the levels on which paid sex with Miles Davidson—and she may as well call it that, because that's what it was, prostitution pure and simple—the levels on which it would leave its mark were the deepest levels of her being. One screen test would not be worth it. Even a whole career could not be worth it, and how terrible to find it out too late!

Cady knew all this within a split second. She did not think about it, or reason it out; she simply knew it, all at once. It was a strange and new sensation, as if the fact of loving Luke Southam had put her in touch with her own deep wisdom. It was not like learning, it was like uncovering the truth that she had always known.

"Luke the Healer," she thought aloud.

Beside her Luke moved to kiss her forehead. "Pardon?" he asked.

"Luke was a healer, wasn't he?" she asked. "I mean the original, biblical Luke. Wasn't he a physician?"

"By tradition he is, I guess."

"Hmm." Absentmindedly, for the comfort it gave her, she stroked his chest.

"And what does that mean?" Luke asked with a smile in his voice.

"Oh, I was just thinking."

His chest shook under her hand as he laughed a short, throaty laugh. *I like your laugh*, thought Cady. *It has just the right sound to it.*

"And who was the original Cady?" Luke asked then.

"I've never been exactly sure who I was named after. On my birth certificate my name is Caedmon. Nobody left any record of why I was named that, but when I looked it up I found a historical Caedmon, and I like to think that's who my parents named me after. Have you ever heard of him?"

"It sounds very distantly familiar. . . . Could he be as far back as English Lit 101?"

She smiled. "Probably. Caedmon lived in seventh-century Britain. There used to be a custom at feasts then, that the harp was passed around the table after the meal, so that each guest would entertain the others with a song. But Caedmon felt he couldn't sing or make verse, and he used to disappear out to the stables before the harp got to him.

"One night in the stables a person, a vision appeared to him, surrounded by light, and said, 'Caedmon, sing me a song.' Caedmon fell on his knees, saying something like 'Lord, you know I can't sing, I have a terrible voice, please don't ask me to sing.' But the personage said again, 'Caedmon, sing me a song.' So Caedmon sang a song, a song of creation, and the lady of the manor was sitting upstairs at a window and heard the song. She called for the singer to be brought to her and asked him to sing to her because he had the sweetest voice she had ever heard. And after that, Caedmon became a monk and devoted his life to composing sacred verse."

"Of course," said Luke, remembering. "Caedmon's Hymn."

"Umm-hmm."

"That's a nice story. I don't remember it being so moving."

"Some books make it seem very dry and boring. Venerable Bede wrote about it, but I never read him in the original."

"And you think you were named after that Caedmon? A good namesake for an actress."

She hadn't told Luke much about her adult life, it hadn't seemed important. But he knew that much, that she made her living as an actress.

"It is, isn't it?" she agreed. "And I like the idea of God coming along to point out the talents you've been burying."

"It was God, was it?"

"Wasn't it? Who else?"

"An angel?" he suggested. "A subconscious projection of the inner self?"

"Maybe they're all the same thing, in the end."

"Ah," breathed Luke in his smiling voice. "Now we're getting profound. God as the inner self?"

Tonight she felt she understood everything, with a direct, certain knowledge that seemed to come from her love for Luke. She could not quite express it in words, but she felt as though she knew something deep and mysterious. "Well, everybody's always said God is within you. I mean, what does that mean if it doesn't mean what it says?"

"I don't know. You're making me wish I'd studied theology instead of English 101."

She laughed, and the laugh was interrupted by a yawn. "Oh, boy," she said ruefully, "do we have to make an early start tomorrow?"

"We should if we're going to cover the ground we decided on."

Luke had studied the map of the park and come up with a route out that might be faster than the ones either of them had followed in, by virtue of its having fewer portages and longer trips by water. Part of it was over his own route in. But it would mean one long portage early tomorrow and then a full day's canoeing, and making another short portage before setting up camp. That would get the hardest part over with the first day. Then, with a moderate forcing of their pace, they should make it out of the park in two more days. If they didn't, if Luke's arm wasn't up to it, it would take them an extra day. A hungry extra day, but nothing they couldn't cope with.

"We should stop talking and go to sleep, shouldn't we?" she said.

"Mmm-hmm," agreed Luke. And aware that her heart was unfolding like a flower, Cady curled up against him and slipped down into sleep.

SHE DIDN'T KNOW how Luke made it the first day. On the portage he was loaded, as she was, with a canoe and a backpack and another pack hanging from that. Her aspirins were all gone, as was the first-aid ointment and most of the aloe-vera gel, and his own first-aid kit was nearly as depleted. He was taking half a painkiller every four hours, and she knew that it must be useless against the resurgence of pain caused by exertion. He sweated so much the sweat blinded him until, in exasperation, he ripped a strip from one of his towels and tied it around his forehead.

Once she suggested that they travel in easier stages, to which he responded with a gruff, "Let's just keep going, okay?" She backed off immediately. If he thought he could stand the pace it wasn't her business to tell him otherwise.

The canoeing was much easier, of course, at first. By late afternoon Cady was fading fast, and how Luke could go on she couldn't imagine. Just as she was beginning to think she would rather do a fourth day on short rations than push her paddle one more time they came to the portage point.

"Want to stop?" Luke asked impatiently. They were the first words that had passed between them for what seemed like hours.

"Only if you do," she replied, and for an answer Luke shouldered into his pack and with a gut-wrenching grunt lifted up his canoe.

This portage was mercifully short, and they staggered into the campsite on the new lake just as the sun was setting. By which point Cady was getting punch-drunk. She set down her canoe with an exaggerated groan and straightened, rubbing the small of her back.

"No rest for the wicked," she said. "I hate pitching a tent after dark. Let's get it over with and then rest."

"Right," said Luke shortly, and she eyed him with concern.

"How bad is it?" she asked gently.

"What—my arm?" he asked. "Oh, it's not bad, Cady. There's nothing wrong with my arm."

She didn't believe him. What else could be making him so brusque and short-tempered? He had had no patience all day with the little things that went wrong. If he stumbled on a loose rock, he kicked it out of the way. If the canoe caught on a branch, he swore.

She said, "You sit down. I'll pitch the tent." But without answering Luke bent to untie the tent from his pack and strode over to the small area of cleared ground that was the obvious location for it.

When they had pitched the tent and gathered wood and made a fire, Cady sat beside it opening packages of food while Luke went down to the lake with a saucepan. When he came back, setting it on the fire, he said, "This one's dead."

Startled, Cady looked up. "What?" she gulped. For a wild moment she expected him to be holding a dead animal. He wasn't. "What?"

He was settling the pot in the flames. "The lake," he said briefly. "It's dead."

"Oh!" She jerked her head to look out over the glistening expanse of water, almost black in the dusk now, with a few strokes of gold painted by the dying rays of the sun. "Completely? Everything?"

"I think so," he said. "No fish, plankton, algae, weeds—nothing. You can see right to the bottom—just mud and stones."

"Oh hell!" She wanted to weep; it was too depressing, coming after a full day's exertion, and she had no reserves left. Until now she had hoped against hope that in spite of what she had heard, acid rain could not really have penetrated so deeply into the wilderness, that somehow all the environmentalists were wrong.... "Why don't they stop?" she demanded helplessly. "Why don't they just stop pumping all that stuff into the air—into *our* air?"

Luke looked at her steadily. "We do cause some of it ourselves," he pointed out. "Inco isn't exactly Snow White when it comes to pumping sulfur dioxide into the air."

"I know, but . . . ." Cady moved a hand in a helpless gesture. The tragedy was that sulfur dioxide was no respecter of borders. Pumped into the air at ever higher altitudes by the tall smokestacks that coal-burning industry had developed to protect nearby cities, sulfur dioxide was blown far away from its source to come down in the wilderness areas of the world as sulfuric acid, changing forever the pH balance of lakes in the most beautiful tourist and vacation areas, bringing the most deadly pollution to areas of the world that were otherwise untouched by civilization.

But it was difficult to convince a distant government and distant industry of the need to curb the pollution, of the urgent necessity to preserve for all mankind the northern wilderness of forests and lakes. That industry in the Ohio Valley, for example, could be destroying Northern Ontario's vast beauty, or that sulfur dioxide from industrial Europe could be killing Norway's lakes, was, it seemed, a notion difficult for the perpetrators to accept.

Cady was not the only one who felt a deep and growing bitterness toward those industries who blindly went on with this destruction. Anyone whose livelihood depended on fishing or tourism, anyone who loved the wilderness or even just the knowledge that there were areas of the world still untouched by man, was as deeply affected, and their numbers included large segments of the populations of Canada and Scandinavia, as well as those in the tourist areas of the northeastern United States.

But what Luke was saying, Cady knew, was that it was a global problem that would require global cooperation to cure.

"You're right," she admitted with a helpless shrug, but the knowledge did not ease her bitterness.

That night, as she lay beside him, sore in every muscle, she was surprised to feel him reach for her. Even more surprised by the intensity with which he held her. She had never before felt in him this tension. He had been gentle and loving with her from the beginning.

Suddenly she realized that his brusque mood on the trail had been caused not only by pain, but in part by the same feeling that gripped him now.

"Luke, what is it?" she whispered in sudden fear.

He held her tightly, stroking her face and then her arm, and her flesh cleaved to his touch. "You trust me, don't you, Cady?" he asked hoarsely, and under her cheek she felt the perspiration start on his skin. Suddenly her stomach was hollow with fear.

She did trust him. My God, how she trusted him—he had crept in under her guard day by day. She hadn't known how much until this moment, when he was going to tell her that trusting him was a mistake.

"Yes, I trust you, Luke," she said, almost without breath, and it was the same as saying "I love you." But already she was retreating inside, already her heart was running for cover, the old familiar cover that had protected her from childhood. "Why? Shouldn't I?"

"Yes," he ground out, "yes, my God, you should, Cady, but I—" He broke off, breathed deeply and began again. "If it was anyone else I wouldn't— But you're so vulnerable, I'm afraid you'll see it as—" Another deep breath, another beginning. "Cady, I've got something to tell you. I should have told you before, I should have told you right away, but the time never seemed right, and I—I kept thinking there'd be a better time. . . ."

Funny how quickly a half-unfolded flower could close up and become a lump of ice. Especially while the tears on your cheeks were so hot.

Whatever he had to tell her could only mean one thing, and she suddenly didn't want to hear it one moment earlier than she had to. With an instinct that surprised her, she covered his mouth with her hand and cried into the darkness, "Then don't tell me, Luke, not yet! We've still got another two days. It's— I haven't expected anything more than that, anyway—" oh, the lies that could come to your throat when inside you were dying! "—I knew it would be over when we left the park, Luke. Let's have the next two days, Luke, it's all right, I understand, but please don't tell me yet—"

His anguished kiss smothered her words in her throat then, and his hands on her body were more demanding than she had ever felt them; her response was a sudden fire that she had never before experienced.

"It's not going to be over, Cady," he said hoarsely when he lifted his mouth. "I am not going to let myself lose you through my own damn stupidity. I can't afford to lose you, are you listening to me? I can't lose you now!"

He pulled up her fleecy top and stroked her breast with one trembling hand—his burned hand, but he seemed to have forgotten his burn.

"You are beautiful to me," he said hoarsely. "You are so blindingly beautiful to me that I don't even know whether you are beautiful to other men. Are you beautiful by the world's standards, too?"

"Yes," she whispered, for it was of no importance.

The urgency of his hand on her was a flame set to the gunpowder of her blood, and she lay against him in mute surprise as her desire mounted higher and higher.

"Yes," he repeated. "I wish you weren't. From the first moment I saw you I've— My God, what a fool I've been. What a fool I'm being. Am I scaring you?"

"No," she choked. It was no lie, it wasn't he who terrified her, but the overwhelming response of her mind and body to the assault of his need of her.

He kissed her again, deeply and powerfully, holding her head with both hands. "Tell me you'll listen to everything I have to say when I do tell you," he ordered. "If I don't tell you now, promise me you'll listen when I do."

"Yes," she said, "yes, I pro—" She broke off with a

gasp as his hand began to stroke her, pushing the fabric of her track suit out of the way.

"I've been so gentle with you," he whispered as his hand moved against her and he listened avidly in the darkness for her response. "I should have known I'd crack. Don't be afraid, Cady."

She was long past fear; she had moved into a realm of pure sensuality that she had never guessed existed. "Ah! Luke, don't," she protested then, as his hands and his mouth drew her down to where nothing mattered save the pleasure he gave her, and some part of her mind fought to retain control. "Oh my God, Luke, don't, don't, you— Ohhh . . ." she breathed, as the first of the pleasure he would give her flooded through her being, and she opened herself to him with an abandon so complete it seemed closer to death than to life.

"That's it," his voice rasped approvingly in her ear. "Don't say don't, Cady. I want to feel you tremble, let me make you tremble."

She could form no word but his name, and when his powerful body moved at last to claim hers she repeated his name over and over with every stroke of pleasure that he gave her.

"Cady," he whispered urgently at last. "Cady, stop. When you say my name like that I can't—"

"Luke," she moaned, and the tight knot of pleasure within her burst up through her body like a shooting spiral, and her voice broke with surprise so that suddenly it was with a deep growl that she called to him, over and over, "Luke, Luke, Luke!" She shuddered and clutched at him with a strange fierce desperation as the pleasure coursed through her. Then she felt the arch of his neck as Luke threw back his head and cried out her name in a voice that was flooded with the surprise of the most profound pleasure he had ever known.

LATE ON SATURDAY AFTERNOON they canoed across the glinting surface of the last lake, and came in sight of the landing stage and the warden's station that would be their last stop before the park gates.

The weather had got suddenly cooler, and Cady and Luke both wore down vests over warm sweaters. The last day's journey had been relatively easy, but somehow during the last hour as they paddled side by side a silence had fallen between them: the silence of knowing that every stroke of their paddles brought them closer to the moment when Luke would have to tell her what he did not want to tell her and what Cady did not want to hear.

When at last he maneuvered closer to her and shipped his paddle her heart was beating with something like terror. She lifted her own paddle and looked mutely at him as Luke reached out to hold her canoe against his.

"Cady," he said quietly, matter-of-factly, "I live with a woman. I've been living with her for just over two years. We—" he took a deep breath "—we've been talking about getting married."

She was as stunned as if he had hit her openhanded across her face with all his strength. She stared at him, feeling some invisible agent stretch all the skin of her face until it felt as though she had been burned in a fire and the scar tissue was hideously smooth and taut.

He saw the look and squeezed his eyes shut against it. "Trust me," he pleaded. "Trust me."

Cady said nothing, all her concentration on the knives that had once stabbed her heart at the thought of Margery Simpson's pain and that were stabbing her again now, with a hundred times greater sharpness.

He said, "We were only talking about it. Sharon— that's her name, Cady—Sharon would like to have children, and my sister and one brother are married, and she . . . it seemed like a good idea, Cady, only I'm not—

I wasn't sure. I thought—love, my God, isn't there more than this? Doesn't there have to be more than. . .I love her, Cady, I'm fond of her, but I didn't see how it was going to last all our lives. . . .''

For a writer, Luke thought, he wasn't doing very well with narrative. Hell, why hadn't he told her right away? He had always thought that the right time would come, and then, suddenly, he had run out of time.

He should have made her listen Thursday night, he could see that now. He could have held her and explained, and waited all night for her reaction, if necessary. Why had it seemed so easy to put it off then, when it seemed so wrong now?

"Cady, do you understand what I'm telling you?"

"Yes, of course." Her face mirrored an absolute calm. She was more composed than he had ever seen her. With anyone else he would have felt relieved, but Cady was always so vital, so alive, that her calm now alarmed him, as though he were in the presence of death.

What a crippler of the tongue guilt was. He kept hearing his father's voice saying, "Never be dishonorable in your dealings with any woman, Luke. If you use one woman with dishonor, how can you promise another that you'll treat her right and expect to be believed?" It was probably all old-fashioned, chauvinistic trash, but he couldn't get the voice out of his head. Anyway, old-fashioned or not, it was true at this moment. He was tied up in the knot of knowing that he had not treated Sharon, and therefore Cady, fairly.

He said, "I wanted to think it over. I needed time. It was like—Cady, I was. . .I think I was going to agree, I think I was coming out here to say goodbye to something, to learn to settle for what I had, to give up on the dream. . . . And then there you were. . . . Cady, do you understand?"

Her heart was a stone; she was impervious to everything. She looked at him, conscious of nothing more than a dim pity for his obvious discomfort. "Luke," she said, picking up her paddle, "don't worry about it. It doesn't matter."

"Cady, I loved you the moment I looked at you."

"That's all right, Luke. I know. I loved you, too. It's okay. It's really okay."

Then why did he have the feeling that he was looking at disaster? Her pleasant, understanding calm wasn't reassuring at all, but he didn't know why. This was a ridiculous situation anyway. Two canoes. He was having the most important conversation of his life in two canoes. Luke snorted in wry amusement, and when Cady put her paddle in the water he didn't argue.

"Look," he said, "we can't discuss this here. Let's get out of the park and find a restaurant in Huntsville where we can have a decent dinner, okay?"

It would choke her to swallow a mouthful. She didn't want to eat or talk, she just wanted to get as far away from him as possible, she just wanted to be alone. She was okay, everything was okay, but she needed to get away from here.

Cady put her paddle in the water and pulled easily away from him. Oh, well, there was no point in making a fuss, one more meal with him wouldn't kill her. Anyway, she had known all along that it was temporary.

"Sure," she called across the widening space of water between them.

"Do you know Hunter's, just off the highway as you're driving into Huntsville?"

"Is it still there?" she said. "Sure, I know it."

"Let's eat there. If we lose each other on the road I'll see you there."

Her stomach was clenching and heaving, though she didn't know why. Cady began to paddle harder. "All right. Last one there pays for dinner!"

CADY DROPPED OFF THE SILVER CANOE at the small store in Huntsville where she had rented it, but there was no refund for returning it a day early. Then she took to the road again. It wasn't till she found herself heading south on the highway instead of back to the turnoff for Hunter's restaurant that she knew she wasn't going to meet Luke. Up till then she had thought she would, she had really thought she could stand to listen to his explanations. Only as she picked up the north-south highway and felt her body take a deep involuntary breath did she realize how much she had been dreading that explanation.

Distantly she wondered what he had been going to tell her. That he would need time to think? That he wouldn't have cheated on Sharon unless he had been having doubts or feeling pressured or whatever it was? That now he loved two women?

She was glad she hadn't stuck around to hear it. She might have ended up—what? Begging? Throwing a glass of wine in his face? Something awful. If she knew one thing by now, it was that her feelings would always lead her into trouble. Only when she controlled them was she safe.

She would feel more herself once she got back to Toronto. If she drove nonstop she would arrive an hour or so after Thea's late show came down. Thea wouldn't be expecting her tonight, but that wouldn't matter. She would rather push it and go all the way home tonight than stop off at a motel. She needed to feel at home just this once. She needed to feel that there was somewhere where she belonged and was welcome. She needed company.

Oh, please, let Thea not be throwing a party tonight.

Cady drove well, if sometimes a little hesitantly. This trip was her first experience of driving in Canada after six years in England, and it still seemed odd to be sitting in the left-hand seat and driving on the right, instead of vice versa. But driving in Canada was a lot easier than in England, with its twisting roads and its traffic circles, and soon she was putting her foot down, traveling at that finely judged speed that was above the speed limit but below the speed at which a traffic cop would bother to flag you down.

She was tired. Her arms ached, her back ached, her head was thumping behind her eyes. After three hours of driving Cady was forced to stop for coffee, but she drank two cups in ten minutes and hit the road again.

Traffic was light in Toronto, but it was long after midnight before she was parking Thea's little blue car in front of her Cabbagetown apartment with a sigh of relief.

She had driven the whole way without thinking. That was good; it must be some kind of record. Cady unlocked the front door, dragged herself up the stairs to Thea's apartment and let herself in.

Darkness. "Thea?" she called, flicking on the hall light. But there was no answer. "Oh, no," she whispered softly. "Don't be out tonight, Thea, not tonight."

She walked through the apartment to Thea's bedroom, flicking on lights as she went, but though the bed was in violent disorder, it had the air of an old disorder: Thea rarely made her bed, and she hadn't been in it tonight.

Standing at the bedroom door, Cady suddenly slumped, in body and spirit. Leaning against the doorjamb she closed her eyes and bit her lip and tried not to let the loneliness swamp her.

God, how empty she was, how achingly lonely. Just at this moment she felt lonelier than she had ever felt in her life, except perhaps the night her parents had died.

She could feel the horror rising like bile in her throat. With a determined breath Cady turned back into the living room and flicked on the television. She would have to wait up for Thea. There was no way she was going to sleep tonight. She couldn't sleep, not tonight, not alone in this empty apartment, in her empty life, in an empty world.

The tears were beginning now, and the clenching in her stomach was turning into deep sobs. Biting her lip, Cady ran into the bathroom and began running a bath. The radio went on as she flicked on the bathroom light, and that was good. Noise was what she needed, noise going in her ears to push down her inner voices, drown them out.

She stripped there, standing in the middle of the bathroom, and crawled into the scalding water, which reddened her skin and made her gasp.

When she turned off the noisy taps the voice of the late-night disc jockey on Thea's favorite station met her ears, warm and intimate, a voice designed to fool lonely people into believing they were not alone. She became abruptly aware of the fraud, and suddenly she was hating the voice and all the memories it raised in her. All her life there had been someone who had tried to convince her she was not alone—her grandparents, social workers, the odd teacher and foster parent. And now Luke. And she had always swallowed it, to some extent. She had swallowed it because she had needed to believe it. She had needed to believe that someone cared, that there was someone for her to love.

Every time she had let herself believe what they told her, every time, the lie had caught up with her. They had left her, or betrayed her, or let her be taken away. . . .

It was all a lie, it always would be. Cady had always known it, and still had let herself be lulled each time into believing. But she wasn't going to be fooled again. Not by the Lukes of the world, not by the phony radio voices. She was alone, she would always be alone. And she knew it.

Cady stood up decisively and pulled the plug to let the water out. Wrapping a towel around her, she snapped off the light, silencing the radio voice, and went on into the living room to turn off the television. She did not need noise to get her through anything. She didn't need anyone.

In the room that Thea had converted to a bedroom for her, the same one that used to be her bedroom when she had shared the apartment six years ago, she dried herself off and slipped into pajamas, brushed the braids out of her long black hair and slid into bed. She lifted her arm to the bedside lamp. Nothing would ever get to her again. She would never again let someone get in under her guard the way Luke had done. Never. From now on she would look after herself. With a small nod and a satisfied grunt, Cady flicked out the light and settled herself for sleep.

Two hours later she woke up screaming.

LUKE HAD EVERY INTENTION of paying for dinner, so he didn't hurry. Anyway, his arm could do with the rest. It wasn't till he saw the little silver canoe through the trees, whipping along the road on top of a blue car while he was still in the parking lot tying his canoe to the roof of his own car, that a sense of urgency gripped him. Suppose she couldn't remember how to find Hunter's after all? She had told him it had been a few years since she was here last. Suppose she changed her mind? She had been so calm after what he'd told her. Suppose she hadn't been falling in love with him at all when he thought she was?

Luke snapped the last knots into the rope and threw his packs unceremoniously into the car. It took him only a minute to locate the ignition key he had thrown

under the front seat, but by the time he set off Cady had
had a few minutes head start. Enough to get away if that
was what she wanted.

Luke hit the road at speed, the sense of urgency not
letting go of him no matter how much he tried to reassure himself that Cady had promised to eat dinner
with him. He drove as fast as he could on the curving,
hilly highway, but he never caught sight of a blue car
with a silver canoe on its roof.

Nor was it in the parking lot of Hunter's restaurant,
which he reached as darkness fell. Well, perhaps she had
missed the turnoff. Perhaps she would come back. She
had to come back.

Luke found a parking space that faced the road and
sat in his car, waiting for the sight of the silver canoe.

"Hell," he said aloud, "I don't even know the make of
the car. I wish I'd—" Suddenly he broke off and hit the
steering wheel. "My God, Cady!" he cried aloud, his
voice a hollow, horrified plea. "My God, I don't know
your last name! Cady, your name, my God, my God,
what's your *name*?"

5

FOR A WEEK her days and nights were such a jumble of memory and dream Cady could scarcely tell the difference. Whether she was awake or asleep her mind was full of faces, names, snatches of remembered conversation that tormented her constantly. Her parents, her grandparents, her friend Shirley, Margery Simpson and all the others whom as a child she had loved and lost—one after another, they smiled and turned away. Their faces filled her dreams as she moved restlessly in her sleep, filled her burning brain as she paced her room and the apartment, afraid, alone, cut off.

She slept and woke at odd hours. Sometimes as she paced she saw sunrise, sometimes a chill cold night and rain, sometimes there was darkness beyond the windows. But she did not know whether she paced, or dreamed that she paced.

Her parents came. They stood side by side, looking down at her sadly. "We love you, Cady. Be a good girl. Goodbye," they said to her. She could not understand. "If you love me why are you going?" she asked pitifully. "If you love me, take me with you, don't leave me, please don't leave me! Please come back!" But they were already far away, moving into the distance as though they were on a spaceship rushing a million miles away from her; and the footsteps had already started their monotonous chilling thud—thud—thud, coming closer and closer to where she lay. The footsteps—she hated the footsteps. They froze her blood, made her heart pound, made sleep impossible.

After a while she learned that that was the distinction between sleeping and waking: if she heard those relentless footsteps she knew she was asleep—and if she woke up screaming.

Even Thea was there, her vivid personality burning through the haze that filled Cady's brain. "Are you all right?" she kept asking. "Are you all right?"

"Why are you here?" Cady asked the vision. "You're not like the others, you never left."

Thea swore helplessly. "Cady, what is it? What's the matter? Are you all right?"

There was some quality about her that was different. In the recesses of her mind Cady pondered the nature of the difference. It took a long, long time, a light-year. "Oh," she said, surprised to find Thea still there after all that time, the same expression of concern on her face, as though she had just finished speaking. "You're not a dream. You're really here. Hi, Thea."

She sensed a sigh of relief. "Hi yourself. What's going on? What's happening with you?"

Some part of her knew she must reassure Thea. "I've been having trouble sleeping," she said. "I'm having nightmares. I'm all right, don't worry about me."

"Do you want me to call a doctor?"

"No," she said. She must be left alone now. There was something she was learning to understand, and she must go on until she did. "I'm all right, Thea. I need to be alone, that's all."

"Okay," said Thea slowly. "I've been over at Bernie's for a couple of days. I'm going back there when I've picked up a few things. You're sure you're all right alone?"

Later, she didn't know how much later, Thea was there again. "I've stocked the fridge," she said. "I don't know what you've been living on, Cady—there wasn't any food anywhere. Try and eat, okay?"

"Okay," she nodded. She thought a while, trying to find the words. "You're a good friend, Thea."

"I'm not so sure," said Thea dryly. "But I'm doing what you say you want me to do. Look, I've put Bernie's telephone number by the phone. If you want anything, Cady, call me there. Call me anytime, Cady, I mean it."

"Yes," agreed Cady, and then a door closed and she was alone. She hated the sound of a door closing. It hit her memory bank like a gunshot, reminding her of all the other doors that had closed during her life, behind people she loved, closed forever.

She cried and paced, cried and paced. "They're gone," she heard the voices say, "they're never coming back." And she cried aloud that same protest that had haunted her childhood. "But I want them to come back! I don't want them to go away forever! I need you, I love you!" And somehow she knew that it was *because* she loved them that they were leaving her. Her need was driving them away. "Don't go, please don't go!" She was back inside the nightmare, enveloped in the anguish that had lived inside her unacknowledged for so many years.

She saw Luke in her dream, getting married to a beautiful black girl. "I am black but beautiful," the woman said when she made her vow, "I am the rose of Sharon."

Luke held out his blistered arm for Cady to bandage. "His left hand is scarred," said the black woman, "but his right hand doth embrace me."

"Goodbye, Cady," said Luke, and then her head was filled with a hundred voices, all echoing goodbye... goodbye...goodbye....

Thud...thud...thud. "No footsteps!" screamed Cady, waking herself up. "No footsteps!"

Suddenly she was wide awake. It was broad daylight,

and she was sweating little cold beads of water that had drenched the pillow and the sheets and her clothing.

Her clothing. She was wearing a wrinkled green shirt and khaki trousers, which she had no recollection of having put on, and she was ravenously hungry. She gave her head a tentative shake, but there was no sound save the noise of street traffic. The voices were gone.

Cady stood up gingerly and staggered to the bathroom. Reluctantly, she looked in the mirror. What day was it? She was dirty and disheveled, her face showing the marks of countless tears, her hair in a dirty tangle. She looked thin, drained, almost wasted.

Where had she been, and how long had she inhabited that pit of hell? Brushing her tangled hair back with futile motions of her hands Cady approached the phone. "Thea at Bernie's" read the phone pad in large letters, and then the seven digits of a phone number.

Cady dialed the operator. "Could you tell me what time it is?" she tried to ask, but her voice was so hoarse she had to try three times before she could speak. "Also, what day is it?"

"I'm sorry, madam," came the impersonal, singsong voice. "I am a Bell operator. I don't give out the time."

How could such a small rejection hurt so desperately? "Look," she whispered, fighting against tears, "just human to human, couldn't you tell me the time? And date?"

"I'm sorry, madam," said the voice again. "I don't have the correct time to give you."

"A rough estimate will do," Cady pleaded. "Don't you have a watch on? Couldn't you just—"

The uncaring voice was like a blunt instrument falling on her terrible fragility.

"I'm sorry, madam."

"Well, the day, then. Could you at least just tell me what day it is?"

There was a shocked pause. Then, "It's Saturday."

"Saturday!" Cady croaked, amazed. She looked out the window to where the sun was shining. How could it be Saturday? She had driven down from Algonquin on Saturday! "Are you sure?"

The voice was growing distinctly cool. "Yes, I'm sure. Saturday."

"Saturday, what date?"

Another pause. "I don't think I should be talking to you," said the operator coldly. And Cady knew that it was her need that was driving the woman away, her need for human contact. "Look," she said desperately, "please don't hang up. Please. I've been sick...." She searched for something ordinary, something the woman would understand. "I must have been delirious, I lost track of time. Please, what is the date?"

In a concerned but still-guarded tone the woman said, "Saturday, October 15. I think you should call a doctor, dear."

"Thank you, I will," Cady assured her. "I really will."

She moved back to the bathroom and stripped off her damp, clammy clothes. *The fifteenth*, she thought dumbly, her tears never very far away. *October the fifteenth. I came back on the eighth. That makes it a week. Seven days of being completely out of my mind.*

IN THE AFTERNOON, Cady phoned Miles Davidson's office. It was Saturday, but when you wanted to be the next boy wonder in Hollywood, you didn't keep office hours.

But it was a surprise to find his secretary-assistant in. "He's in L.A.," this young woman offered when she asked for Miles. "I'm waiting for a call from him sometime today. Do you want to leave a message?"

"Still in L.A.?" asked Cady in surprise. As far as she knew, he'd been expecting to stay only a few days. He ought to have been back two weeks ago.

"Not still. Again," said the secretary, a woman Cady knew only as Kit.

"Kit, it's Kate Hunter," she said.

"Oh, hi, Katie, you're back. How was your holiday?" Both Kit and her boss were American, and when they said "Katie" it was nearly indistinguishable from "Cady." The English had always pronounced the *t* in Katie very precisely, a constant reminder to her of the change she had made in her name. It was distinctly pleasant to hear the sound of her own name after so many years, like wearing your favorite old slippers after a long time in firm leather oxfords.

"Super," Cady responded, injecting a warmth into her voice that would have fooled anyone. "We had absolutely gorgeous Indian-summer weather. I swam nearly every day."

"Wow," said Kit admiringly. "You must belong to the Polar Bear Club!"

Kit was easy to talk to now that Cady was so close to being cast in a major role; she had got progressively more friendly as Cady had moved through the screenings and auditions, as though Cady's worth was being defined by Miles Davidson's estimation of her talent. It was the sort of thing that irritated Cady when she ran into it. But it was an attitude that was rife in the film world, if not in theater, and if she wanted to make the shift she had better get used to it. She did not let herself dwell on it.

"So how come Miles is back in L.A.?" she asked after a few minutes.

"Oh, nothing to worry about," Kit said lightly, in a voice of slightly forced nonchalance that sent an immediate chill of alarm up Cady's spine. "A little hitch, but Miles will straighten it out. Not to worry. He'll be back in a couple of days, he'll call you. Not to worry."

Thea came through the door just as Cady was hanging up. "Great!" Cady told her without preamble. "Miles Davidson has been called back to L.A.! I suppose one of the producers wants his little friend to have a part in the film—*my* part, of course!"

"*Your* part, is it?" Thea said with a broad grin, pulling off her chocolate-colored tam and flinging it onto the sofa. "So where did you hear all this juicy gossip?"

Cady grinned sheepishly. "Well, actually, I didn't hear it anywhere. I'm just assuming that's why he's back in L.A. It seems fitting—just when I'd decided to get that part whatever way I had to."

Thea shrugged out of an outsize army jacket without taking her eyes off Cady. "You decided, didja?"

She had decided, though she couldn't have said when. Perhaps in the split second after Luke Southam had said to her, "I live with a woman." What a fool she had been, letting a meaningless affair get to her so deeply, take on an importance it never had. If she could sleep with Luke Southam she could sleep with Miles Davidson. There was really no difference. She had imagined herself in love with Luke; she could imagine herself in love with Miles.

Thea led the way into the kitchen, where she started poking around in the fridge for the makings of a meal. "Is that what last week was all about?"

Cady shook her head as she took plates down from the cupboard. "No," she said, "last week—well, it was kind of weird."

"Mmm," Thea agreed, sucking a morsel of pâté off her thumb. "I'll say it was. You scared me—crying and sweating and shrilling at me to leave you alone."

"Did I? I don't remember that."

"Well, I'll never forget it. If I didn't have such faith in the natural healing process of the mind you'd have freaked me right out. But you really seemed to be working through something, so I left you to it. I came in once a day to make sure you were alive. That's what I'm here for now—I told Bernie I'd only be a while. It's great to have you back to normal." She sliced tomatoes and onions into a small salad and sprinkled her own potent garlic dressing over the top.

Meanwhile Cady pulled out bread and butter and crackers and some sliced meat. Her stomach growled suddenly, and she felt overwhelmingly hungry. "Gosh, I feel as though I haven't eaten for a week!"

Thea was putting out some cheese. "You probably haven't," she said, eyeing Cady. "I stocked up when I knew you were home, but before that there wasn't much in the fridge. You don't seem to have made inroads on anything I bought, either."

She had never been as hungry as this in her life. Cady fell to as soon as they sat. "I think I drank milk," she said around a large mouthful of bread and cheese.

When the first pangs of her hunger were assuaged, she broke their companionable silence with, "So who's Bernie?"

"Ah, you remembered." Thea smiled. "Bernie. Well, Bernie is my latest. Bernie is an absolute darling. Bernie, in fact, is Bernard Lowe."

"Oh, really!" Bernard Lowe was a well-known stage actor who was currently starring at the Royal Alex in a one-man play that was somewhat derivative of *Krapp's Last Tape*. The play had been panned unmercifully, but no one had denied the actor's talent. "How did that happen?"

"He came to our late show one night after his show came down." Thea shrugged and slid a slice of tomato onto her tongue. "That was, let's see, a week ago today." She grinned. "Things happened pretty fast."

"No kidding." Cady smiled back. "You've been staying at his place all week?"

It seemed as though things had happened as fast for

Thea as they had for her. Funny, Cady thought distantly, how Thea's love affair had begun just as hers had ended. Perhaps there just wasn't enough love in the world to go around? Maybe there was only a tiny little bit of love in all the world? That seemed likely. And she had held on to it for two weeks in Algonquin Park, and now it had flown off to light on Thea.

That must be the way it was. She had had two years at the beginning of her life, and just now she had had ten days, and she would probably never experience it again. Two years and two weeks was a long time to be happy, though, when you considered there must be four billion people in the world, all waiting their turn.

Some of them, those growing up to war or starvation perhaps, would never get their share. They would probably never know love or happiness at all. When you looked at it that way, Cady was one of the lucky ones. She was really amazingly lucky, if you thought about it.

"And we haven't got tired of each other yet!" Thea was saying. "I think I'm in love. Have you ever been in love, Cady?"

Cady flinched.

"What's wrong?" She heard Thea's voice go sharp with concern. "Cady, what is it? What's the matter? You're as white as— Are you in pain?"

Cady could hear the voice, but the questions didn't seem to be directed at her. They didn't seem to require an answer. She was too far away for the questions to be relevant, anyway. She was deep inside herself, choking with a pain against which there was no defense.

"Cady! Answer me! Can you talk?"

The voice was so insistent. Cady blinked at the person standing over her. It was a woman with short, sandy-colored hair, wavy and swept back off her face in a casual style. She had small but expressive eyes, a large nose and mouth. Her face was crinkled up, her eyes full of fear, her lips moving forward and back over her teeth as she opened and closed her mouth. A sound struck Cady's ears each time the mouth moved.

How strange. She hadn't realized that movement caused sound like that. The woman's tongue moved up and down and back, too, curling and stretching. It was making a noise too.

"Cady!" There was a sudden stinging pain in her cheek, a dull ache in her jaw, and her head snapped around. *"Cady, answer me, dammit!"*

"Oh, Thea!" Cady put up her hand to rub her jaw. "I'm sorry! I don't know what happened to me."

Thea's breath rushed out in relief. "God, girl, you looked like death. You didn't have a heart attack, did you?"

That was quite amusing, really. If only it hadn't been so scary. In a way she *had* had a heart "attack," hadn't she? Cady giggled a little.

"Don't get hysterical," Thea begged. "Please, I didn't like hitting you *that* much."

"Sorry," she said. "Sorry." She wiped her hand across her eyes. "I'm all right, I'm not going to have hysterics."

"Cady, what's it all about? What's happened to you? I shouldn't have left you last week, I should have stayed with you, but I thought—"

"Thea, it's all right. Stop worrying, I'll be all right," she said calmly. But she didn't feel calm. She felt suddenly terrified, at the mercy of forces she didn't understand and probably couldn't control. "Could we talk about something else? Something sane and ordinary? *Please.*"

Thea looked at her as though she didn't know what to do. "I'll be okay," Cady said desperately. She wanted to return to sanity, not be forced to talk about Luke. Her pleading gaze locked with Thea's concerned one.

"I could tell you about Augie's latest revolting activities," Thea suggested finally. Augie was one of the actors in the show with Thea, her long-standing pet peeve. Augie liked to upstage his fellow actors. Lots of actors like to do so, of course. But Augie Blake pulled out all the stops. Everyone agreed that Augie took the art to new heights. Or depths.

"I swear he's going to flash the audience one day during that routine we have," Thea had told her, bringing Cady up-to-date on all her news when she had arrived from London. "He's already mooned them, but that's nothing. He'd throw up center stage if he could manage it." She had been only half joking.

"What's he been doing?" Cady demanded now. She had seen the show twice, but neither performance had been enlivened by anything above the general run of upstage techniques.

"You won't believe it," Thea promised her. "I don't believe it myself. In his first routine—you know, he does that crazy political speech right at the top—he gave himself gray hair at the sides. He's done it before—nothing wrong with that. But when he came on next, in the hospital skit, he had made *half* his hair gray, and given himself a wrinkle or two. In his *next* bit, he was really getting old." Thea shook her head. "Every time he came onstage he'd aged himself a bit more. Well, you know what happened: the audience started to watch for it. They were waiting for him to come on so they could check on his progress. If he didn't have a line to say in a skit they'd be waiting for him to move his little finger. The rest of us couldn't get a real laugh out of them to save our lives—you know audiences! He was the star of every scene."

Cady nodded, fascinated. She did know audiences. This was no dramatic exaggeration: after his fourth or fifth appearance the audience would be getting restless and inattentive, whispering to one another, waiting only for Augie Blake to come back with another ten years added to his life. It would be hell on the actors, for no amount of work could call that audience back. For a way to upstage an entire cast, it was not far short of genius, and admirably suited to the comedy-revue genre. He couldn't have done it in a play.

"Well, by the last skit—" Thea was still venting outrage "—he was a doddering old idiot: a head of white hair, crepey white skin, horrible teeth, crippled hands and an interesting tremor! I swear, Cady, they applauded! They thought they were seeing great art! 'What a transformation'—I could hear them thinking that!"

Cady's lips twitched in spite of herself. She wouldn't want to be onstage with Augie Blake herself, but it *was* funny. "Inventive, isn't he?" she commented. "I'd like to know how he did it, too—I've played old women in rep a few times and the makeup took me hours to do." She paused. "He had to have it planned in advance, really, didn't he? It wasn't a spur-of-the-moment thing at all. I don't think I like Augie Blake very much—why don't the rest of you tar and feather him?"

"Good idea," agreed Thea tartly. "I'm getting close to it, I'm telling you. That boy is going to end up with Krazy Glue in his shorts one night if he's not careful."

Thea began to laugh almost against her will, and Cady joined in, shaking her head. "You gotta laugh," Thea admitted. "But it's not very funny when it happens. Until that idiot joined the show I enjoyed every night of work, Cady. We had a real ensemble spirit, we changed the show every night. But the show's been dying—ever since he took over from John. If that guy doesn't straighten out soon...."

Cady said, "Why don't the rest of you plan an ensemble revenge? Why don't you all get *him* one night—

every night till he cries for mercy? You do so much improvisation in that show it should be easy enough."

"Yeah," breathed Thea slowly, getting a light in her eye. "Like how, do you think?"

"Heckle him during that political number, for a start." Cady starting improvising suddenly. "Carry political signs that block him from the audience. Or have a conversation on the 'convention floor.' Or all three."

"A conversation that starts low so they'd have to strain to hear," Thea added, getting the creative spark. "Get the front rows snickering so that everybody wants to know what's so funny! He wouldn't know what the hell was going on! Oh, I can taste this!"

Suddenly her mouth pursed up, and with a sniff she looked at an imaginary someone who was standing beside her. "What's going on?" she hissed out of the side of her mouth. "When is he gonna start taking off his clothes?"

Cady began to laugh. "I think I can see what's coming," she told Thea in delight. She felt a twinge of envy for any actor who could improvise freely, and Thea was the best. Cady herself never felt totally comfortable unless she had a playwright's lines to deliver, and however well she did that, she knew the lack of improvisational freedom was a failing.

Thea was still at it, shifting irritably in her chair. "I ain't waitin' around here all night for this guy!" she muttered threateningly, her voice a fraction louder. "Is he taking them off or not?" She showed all the earmarks of a woman taking courage from her own outspokenness. Her voice began to get perceptibly louder with every line. "I paid fifteen bucks for my ticket, and I ain't waitin' all night!" she went on, a unique vision of self-righteous consumerism and frustrated voyeurism conjoined. She got louder and louder, until finally she was on her feet shrieking, "C'mon, boy, let's see it! Let's see whatcha got! I got a right to see!"

Suddenly she subsided, and the outraged working-class housewife was again Thea. "Well?" she asked Cady.

"I'm beginning to feel sorry for Augie already," Cady confessed, giggling. "He won't last halfway through something like that."

"No, he won't, will he?" Thea agreed with relish. "Hell, I can't imagine why we didn't think of this ourselves long ago."

"Probably because you are an ensemble and too used to team playing," Cady suggested. "But you've thought of it now."

A martial light was aglow in Thea's eyes. "Yes, we have," she agreed. "We sure as hell have thought of it now."

"Luke!" The young woman turned from the bookshelf where she was holding a couple of bound manuscripts and smiled her happy surprise. "How are you? Where have you been?" She threw the manuscripts onto an empty space and walked over to kiss his cheek. "What have you been doing lately?"

He kissed her cheek in return. "Oh, just slogging away, as usual. You're the one with the exciting life these days." He searched his head for some small talk, but found none. His errand seemed too pressing to be delayed. Luke glanced around the empty office. "Could you do me a favor?" he asked abruptly.

"Sure. Of course," she assured him. "What is it?"

"I'm looking for an actress," he said. "All I know about her is that she works out of Toronto. Her name is Cady."

"As in Katherine?" The woman moved back toward the bookshelves. "What's her last name?"

"No, as in Caedmon. And I don't know her last name."

"As in *what*?"

"Caedmon." He spelled it. "She calls herself Cady, C-A-D-Y, but I don't know what name she uses on-stage."

"Well, it's certainly unusual enough. You won't have any trouble tracking that down. You do know what she looks like, I take it?"

"Tall, black hair, blue eyes, very beau—"

He was interrupted by her laughter. "Does Sharon know about this?" she asked, grinning, and Luke winced. The girl sobered in sudden surprise. She had been joking. "Oh!" she said. "I see. Well, there's no point in describing her to me. I see so many actresses every day they all start to look alike." She bent to pull a thick cardboard-bound volume off a shelf. "Canadian, I take it?"

He nodded.

"Established? By that I mean, she has actually worked as a professional actress? She's not a daydreaming secretary?"

"No, I'd say she's been working for a few years, anyway."

She carried the book over to a low table in front of a sofa in one corner of the pleasantly decorated office. "Well, here's *Face to Face*," she offered. "Everybody in the country is in this, if they've worked professionally even once, I sometimes think. But I can't let you take it away, Luke, we need it. Have you got time to go through it now?"

He made an involuntary move toward the book, a move she caught out of the corner of her eye. "I see you have," she said slowly, almost sadly. "Well, you're welcome to sit here for as long as it takes."

Now that what he wanted was within easy reach he

could afford to prolong the agony a little. "Nothing happening?" he asked lightly, as he crossed to sit on the sofa. "Where's Dee?"

Face to Face with Talent read the cover, and Luke couldn't help grinning down at it. *Cady, Cady,* he was thinking, *thank God you are in one of the visible professions. What would I do if you were an accountant?*

"Dee is out of town," the girl said significantly. "*Un*scheduled."

Luke was quick to pick up on it. "Problems?" he inquired with a raised eyebrow.

The girl nodded, her dark brown curls bobbing with the movement of her head. "I think so," she said in a concerned voice. "Between you and me and the gatepost, I think we got trouble."

Luke made an interested face. "That's kind of surprising at this stage, isn't it? What kind of trouble?"

"I don't know," she said, shrugging. "I think trouble can come at any stage. We're talking about an awful big budget, you know."

"Oh," breathed Luke, leaning back against the cushions and eyeing her interestedly. "Money troubles."

The girl grinned her broad engaging grin and tried not to look worried. "Anyway," she said, "I shouldn't be talking about it, even to you. You know how rumors get around. Dee would kill me if it was anyone else. Since it's you I guess he'll just boil me in oil for a bit."

Since "Dee" was a nickname that had been given to his friend in honor of his moodiness—being, as one of the man's ex-girlfriends had once explained to Luke, a short form of both Deity and Diablo—Luke knew that what the girl said now wasn't entirely a joke. "My lips are sealed," he assured her.

"Coffee?" she asked him. "I just made fresh. It should be ready now."

"Great stuff, coffee," said Luke, which answer she

took as an affirmative. She brought him a cup of coffee and set it down on the table beside the book, where he sat staring at the cover. Then she left him alone with the book of photographs and names. The book that would have Cady in it.

"WHAT ARE YOU DOING NOW?" asked the wide-faced blond director when Cady had finished the reading and set the book down.

"I'm not working yet," she told him. She hated the term "resting," and in any case she wasn't sure if it was used in Canada. "I've only just got back from England."

"Mmm," he grunted and made a note on her résumé that lay, with her photograph, on the table in front of him. "You've done a lot of classical stuff, I see," he said at length. "I guess you can do modern, can you?"

Cady grinned at him, ready to share the joke, but the bland, slightly anxious face of the young man was not smiling. He meant it, she realized suddenly. That had been a serious question!

"Well, they say if you can act Shakespeare you can act anything," she said faintly.

She was amazed by the audition process in this country, as well as by the attitude of people to her résumé. "You've forgotten," Thea had told her. "You've forgotten the cult of mediocrity in this country. People don't like anyone to be successful in theater here, remember?"

Cady had listened to her, but she hadn't believed it. Yet the more of her fellow artists she met, the more she was having to give credence to Thea's theory. When other actors heard she had come home after six years in England, they made an automatic assumption that she was coming home a failure, and their hearts warmed to her. When it became clear, however, that she had been offered another season at the famous repertory company where she had last worked, but had turned it down, their warmth cooled and she knew she wasn't imagining the who-does-she-think-she-is attitude that crept in.

Friends were different, of course. Her old friends from theater-school days, several of whom were part of Thea's crowd, were glad to see her and happy that she had done so well in England. It was the others—the familiar old faces and the nodding acquaintances she met at parties and in audition rooms—from whom she felt the unaccountable hostility.

She didn't know which was worse—this attitude, or the American one, that said you were nobody until you'd "made it."

Well, at least the Americans would be decently respectful of her classical background, she thought now. It certainly hadn't made Miles Davidson hostile. "Oh! A real actress!" he'd said the first time they'd met. "This girl's an *actress*, Kit," he'd added. "Not just a pretty television face."

When the blank effeminate eyes of the blond director met hers now she could feel that strange hostility again. Her Shakespearean quip had not gone over, and she sighed tiredly.

"Yes," she said clearly. "I think I can do modern. I think an actor can act or he can't act, don't you?"

The man shrugged. "Oh, theory's theory," he said, with the air of a man who has respect only for hard practicalities. "But the proof's in the pudding."

He couldn't even get the clichés right. She laughed lightly. "Well, there's a fair amount of pudding in front of you," she pointed out. "I've been doing moderns fairly regularly, from Harold Pinter to Tennessee Williams."

"Ever done anything Canadian?" he asked.

She shrugged. This was getting a bit ridiculous. "Not since I left Canada six years ago," she said. "Canadian playwrights aren't exactly beating down the doors of English producers, of course."

"Oh, yes," he observed, reading. "You did a David French play here. How did you like it?"

She wondered where this conversation was going. "I liked it," she said easily. Somehow she didn't think she was ever going to work for this man. "How about you?"

He grunted for reply. He said, "We start rehearsals at the end of November. Four weeks rehearsal, and then we open just before Christmas. Would you have any conflict with that?"

"Possibly," she said. "I'm up for a lead in a movie that's tentatively scheduled to start shooting before Christmas."

"When will you know?"

"The director's in L.A.," she said, automatically hiding her worry over the length of time it had been since she had heard from Miles. Cady had long ago become practiced in the indirect lie, in the ways to appear busy and sought-after even when you were desperate for work. Desperation was the kiss of death to actors. The scent of it would put most producers and directors off the greatest talent living, or so the current myth insisted. The most brazen example of the indirect lie Cady had ever heard of had also been the most successful. "I might be able to fit it in," her friend Robert reported having said to a casting director. "But I'd have to know immediately." He had been offered the part that night.

Cady herself had never been so brazen. It had been several years since she had been seriously out of work, in any case. But the skill of appearing much in demand, once acquired, it seemed, never left you. "He's coming back soon to do a second screen test of me," she finished. She shrugged as though this didn't represent life and death to her. "I imagine I'll know fairly quickly after that."

She had succeeded at last in impressing him. A second screen test! A Hollywood movie! She could read the relief behind his impassive countenance. Someone else thought she was talented; he wouldn't have to rely on his own judgment after all.

"I'm doing second readings in a week or so," the director said then. "Will you be free to come in again?"

Cady lifted her shoulders in a "why not" gesture. "Sure," she said. "Sure, I'd like to." This must be her twentieth audition since coming home. They were all the same. Surely she would get used to it soon?

LUKE WAS IN THE MIDDLE of his study, pacing and eating Oreo cookies. He had the bag, a giant economy size, under one arm, and he reached in at intervals to pull out a cookie and absentmindedly munch at it.

That was the way he always thought: he paced the floor and ate Oreo cookies. As a child, some of his greatest inspiration had come straight out of a bag of chocolate Oreos. In those days he hadn't paced; the treehouse he and Hank and Russell had built had been a little too small for pacing. They had sat cross-legged on the floor in those days, the bag of Oreos in the center of the circle.

"We could—munch, munch—go down the ravine and get a bunch of burrs," Hank would suggest, "and— munch, munch—stick them all over Mrs. Owen's poodle."

"We did that last week," Luke would counter, rooting through the sack for a cookie with a little extra filling, "and all she did was take him to the poodle parlor."

"Yeah, but last week— Hey! stop picking out all the best ones! Last week we did it with honey," Russell said ruefully. "It was too easy to wash off. Burrs will be better."

But Luke was getting inspiration. "Wait a minute!" he

said incoherently, his mouth full of cookie. "I've got it!" They watched him expectantly while he chewed and swallowed. "We'll bury little Geordie Jones up to his neck in his sandpile!"

Nowadays, Oreo cookies made the biggest single contribution to his professional life. He had even dedicated a book once "To Mr. Christie, who makes good cookies." When he got stuck in his plot, when his characters got bloody-minded and refused to do his bidding, or when he stumbled into writer's block, Luke did what he was doing now: he paced and he munched.

But today inspiration was surprisingly lacking. "Cady, dammit," he addressed the room, "why don't *you* phone *me*? I, at least, am in the phone book! In fact, I'm the *only* L. Southam listed! Have you forgotten my last name, Cady? But you know the title of some of my stuff—go and look me up." He looked at the phone, munching. "Dammit, woman, I can think of a million ways you could find *me*! Why don't you do it? And why can't I think of any ways to find you?

"Why aren't you in that book, Cady? How come your picture wasn't in that book?"

Luke paced and munched till for the first time in his life he was nearly sick of Oreo cookies. But he got no inspiration.

He rooted in the bag when it was finally empty, making sure no maverick had escaped his fingers, then scrunched it up and dropped it in the wastebasket beside his desk. A basket that had nothing else in it, because since the cleaning lady had last visited, Luke hadn't been able to write a word.

"I'm gonna find you, Cady," Luke said aloud. "I'm gonna find you if it's the last thing I do."

He sounded optimistic, but in his heart of hearts he was afraid. Cady was so fragile, so vulnerable. Suppose she didn't realize she had never given him her name?

Suppose she thought he'd been lying to her, that he didn't love her as he'd said? Suppose she started to believe she'd been a one-night stand after all? How long would it take him to gain her trust a second time?

There was one thought Luke never allowed himself to think. He never let himself wonder what would happen if he never found her at all.

"Do I WANT TO GO to Regina?" Cady asked Thea one afternoon when the latter had dropped back to the apartment to pick up some things. Thea spent at least half her time at Bernie's now, but Cady saw her most days for an hour or two.

"Man, it's getting cold out there," Thea said, raking her hand through her sandy curls and sinking into a chair opposite Cady. "Do you want to go *where*?"

"Regina."

"I doubt it very much," Thea said humorously. "When?"

"Almost immediately, I think. I read for the man nearly two months ago, and apparently his first choice has fallen through. I've been asked to read again and—"

Thea cast her a look. "Regina, almost immediately? For how long?"

"The play closes just before Christmas."

"Thank you, I can answer your question now. The answer is, no, you do not want to go to Regina for six or seven weeks. You'll cut yourself off from everything that's going on here! Besides, you'll freeze your ass off out there, girl! You'll get snowed in and we won't see you again till late spring. You'll miss Miles's film altogether."

Cady laughed. She knew better than Thea the violence of Saskatchewan winters. She said, "But you know, I think I'll go to the interview anyway. It would do me good to be offered a part now and turn it down. After two months of auditioning I need the ego boost."

"Just be sure you turn it down," Thea advised her. "There's stuff happening in this town—it won't be long before you're offered something a lot better than what George Talousien can offer."

"Lady Macbeth," Cady pointed out.

"Lady Mac?" Thea repeated stupidly. "George Talousien is doing *Macbeth* in *Regina* in the dead of winter? What on—" She subsided comically. "Well, it's been a while since I visited the place, obviously."

"Yeah, me too," said Cady thoughtfully. "Ten years." She was silent, thinking. Ten years. A long time to be away from the province that was her childhood home. She had run away and never gone back, and until those conversations with Luke Southam by the campfire she hadn't realized what a hole that had left in her life. She was tired of being a person without a home, cut off from her own history. So tired that if it hadn't been for Miles Davidson and his damned film, she might have accepted the offer her agent had told her George Talousien was sure to make her.

But it wouldn't do to tell Thea that, she thought, eyeing her friend humorously. With her help and advice Cady had put in a lot of groundwork toward establishing herself in Toronto. Thea wouldn't approve of leaving town before that work paid off.

It began to pay off an hour later, when Cady's agent called.

"More news," she said happily. "They want you for the shampoo commercial!"

It was the first chink of light she had seen for two weeks. Coming after the Regina recall, it was a sign that things were at last moving for her. Cady drew in a huge breath of air and let it out smiling.

"Well, well, well," she said into the mouthpiece. "Finally!"

"Yeah," agreed Patricia. "I told you it was only a matter of time. This is a tight schedule, they want you for Monday. Is that okay with you?"

This was already Friday. It must be a very tight schedule, but Cady wasn't doing anything. . . .

"Oh!" she said. "What about George Talousien, Pat? Isn't he in town Monday?"

"Oh hell, I forgot!" She could hear Pat clinking a pen against her teeth as she thought. "Well, look—he may be staying over Tuesday. I'll call him, try to arrange something. Maybe Monday night. Otherwise you're okay?"

"Free as a bird," sang Cady.

"Get back to you," said Pat, hanging up. She was brusque and businesslike; there wasn't much hand-holding comfort from Pat when things went bad and parts were lost, but she did the job.

"Do I smell a part?" Thea asked when she had hung up.

"A hair commercial—shampoo," she told her. "I've been on so many commercial auditions I can't remember who they were or what I did to get the part."

"Probably you let them look at your hair," Thea said dryly. "It's an advertisement for anything just sitting there. I've always envied you your hair—among other things."

Cady grinned. "Everything but my wit and my comedy talent, right?"

Thea nodded acknowledgment of the point she was making. "All right, all right. Anyway," she said, jumping up, "this calls for a celebration! Is there any wine in the house?"

They pulled out a bottle of plonk and clinked their glasses and drank. "You know, I smell an omen here," Thea said after their first glass. "The theory of threes. You know? You've got one job, another probable offer coming. I think you should phone Miles Davidson and ask him what's happening, don't you?"

Cady made a face. "Oh, I don't know." She felt a deep, heavy resistance to the idea without knowing why. "No, I don't think so, Thea."

Thea shrugged. "Okay, it's your instinct that counts."

But it wasn't instinct that said no. It was the thought of the French River and what a telephone call to Miles Davidson would mean. She had decided to go to the friend's cottage with him, and she was all grown up now and she would follow through on her decision.

But it was too soon after Luke. Luke had used her, and Miles Davidson would use her, and she didn't know how much of that she could take at one time. It would be better to leave it. Let Miles call the timing. Perhaps by the time he got around to calling her she wouldn't feel so sick at the thought of letting him make love to her.

"I think I'll wait," she told Thea easily.

"WELL, WELL, WELL, LUKE! How are you? I understand you've been haunting the place lately, trying to find some girl! What's the matter, you think we're a dating bureau here?" The wide grin belied the words and a friendly hand clasped his own.

"Dee, where the hell have you been?" Luke demanded in humorous exasperation. "I thought you were going to be a fixture in this town for a few months."

Dee pulled a cigarette from his mouth and doused it. "Hey, man," he said with a shrug, "I got troubles. You want to trade your troubles for mine?"

Luke grinned. "Yes," he said.

"Great," said Dee. "Everybody's got bad troubles. So tell me your troubles."

"I'm looking for an actress. I know she lives in Toronto and I know she's been in the business for a few years, and that's all I know. Oh, and I know her first name."

"Some way-to-hell weird name, right? That's what I've been told."

"Cady," supplied Luke. "Short for Caedmon."

"Caedmon," repeated Dee with a snort. "If I ever heard a name less likely to—well, never mind, I won't say it. This is the man sitting here who said Sissy Spacek would never make it." He rolled his eyes heavenward. "Caedmon. Oh, boy."

Luke said, "I've looked through the talent book. She's not there. I want to describe her to you, Dee, maybe you'll remember her."

Dee paused in the act of lighting a cigarette. "You sure you looked through that book thoroughly?" he asked dolefully.

"Ten times, cover to cover," said Luke. "She is not there."

The match burned Dee's fingers and he dropped it and lighted another. Again he paused before lighting his cigarette. "Luke, I gotta tell you, if she's not in that book, man, she just doesn't exist. Everybody goes into that book—makes 'em feel like actors when there's no work. That's like at any given moment, Luke, because—ow! Damn!" He dropped the second match, waved his fingers a little and lit a third.

Before he could speak again Luke said, "C'mon, Dee, there must be some who miss the deadline or forget or haven't got the money or don't want to be in the book for one reason or another."

Dee shrugged and dragged on his cigarette. "All right," he said, "all right. But it's no use describing her to me, Luke, I see a million of these girls. Every day. You know what it's like. Man, if I looked once just at the photos I'm sent through the mail I'd be here till next year."

Luke sat up. "Photos?" he repeated. "You get sent photos through the mail?"

"You're telling me? Man, the press has only got to write one line about somebody being in town or casting a film and he's deluged."

"What do you do with them?" demanded Luke.

"What do you mean, what do I do with them? I told you I don't have time—"

It occurred to Luke that Dee was leading him right down the old garden path. He had been friends with Dee a long time, though often the friendship had been carried on by no more than a postcard or a phone call once a year. During those heady days when Luke was becoming known Dee had written him to ask for film rights to one of his short stories. Luke, with visions of screenwriting greatness in his head, had agreed to do—or insisted on doing, depending on who was telling the story—the screenplay. He and Dee had worked hard to get the project off the ground, but the film had never been made. It was still Dee's favorite unfinished symphony, and he swore he would make the film yet—when the time and place and elements came together. Luke no longer cared about it. If the film hadn't been made, a friendship had. A friendship that had its best foundation, perhaps, in each man's ready sense of humor. Luke looked at Dee.

"All right," he said, "I've been had. You have kindly directed my attention to the hundreds of photos you have got and you know I want to look at them. Where are they?"

Dee grinned and shook his head. "Oh, boy. You better watch it with the broads, Luke, I think your brain is turning to mush."

"Very likely," agreed Luke.

"That filing cabinet behind you has what you've been looking for. It's packed, all four drawers. Don't say I didn't warn you."

Luke got up and pulled open the top drawer. "Good grief," he said faintly.

"By the time you've been through that lot she'll be a

grandmother already," Dee said with relish. "Maybe
now you'll have greater sympathy for my job.

"Look," he said, waving an arm, "take an armload
and go out in the front office, will ya? I got business to
transact, already; if I didn't tell you before, I got
troubles."

"No one deserves them more than you," Luke assured
him kindly, hefting an awkward armload of the slippery
8x11s.

"Hey, listen," Dee's voice arrested him at the door.
"Just out of curiosity, Luke, what *does* she look like?"

"Black hair, blue eyes, a very beautiful tough face,
perfect body," Luke told him.

"Hey, if I did find her I wouldn't give her to you!" Dee
said with a laughing shrug.

Luke looked at him across the width of the office.
There was a stillness in him that few people had ever
had cause to see. Dee had never seen it before, but he
recognized it instantly.

"Yes, you would," said Luke.

6

THE APPLAUSE BEGAN as the lights went down and built to a crescendo as the lights came up again, revealing the cast onstage, smiling, their hands linked.

Augie Blake was not among them, Cady saw at once, which meant he had not taken it well. Well, that was a bully for you, she thought, and Augie Blake was essentially a bully—he could dish it out but he couldn't take it.

The cast had been unmerciful on him, though no one who hadn't seen the show before—or didn't have theatrical experience—would have seen what was going on. They had code-named tonight *R*, for revenge, and by the grins on their faces she could imagine that the revenge had been sweet, if a bit ugly. Augie had taken nothing well. He had at first been bewildered, then shocked—astounded, in fact—then almost frighteningly angry, and finally he had descended into sulkiness. The cast had never let up, although when he began to show his self-righteous anger, it was apparent that he expected to frighten them into stopping. They had only dug into him more cuttingly.

He had deserved it, and then some. When Thea had gone to the cast with her idea of revenge, they had made a decision to try to talk to him first, to reason with him. It hadn't worked. Augie Blake was uncontrollable.

"Well," said one of the actors then, "if we're going to do it, let's do it right." And they had planned a thorough, systematic, slick revenge.

They changed the playing order of several skits so that he was caught unawares. They left out lines that were his cue to enter or speak and carried on without him. They cut his funniest bits of business and killed every punch line he had stone dead. They stood in front of him as though by accident. They rattled bracelets when he spoke. They carried on fascinating sotto voce colloquies in corners, dividing the audience's attention from the main business, which was his. They played whole new scenes in the middle of his skits so that he became an unimportant straight man.

They did that with his very first appearance—as the politician in the second skit of the show. Unbeknownst to him, two front-row seats had been kept back from sale, and Thea and another actress had appeared in the lobby for a while before curtain time, mixing with the audience, acting like two housewives on a special night out, giggly and excitable and feeling very daring. Cady and a few actor friends of the cast had watched them at work, attracting just enough attention to be noticed, out not enough to make anyone suspicious that they were anything other than what they seemed.

During the blackout after the first skit they had slipped into the two front-row seats, and as Augie Blake's speech went on and on, Thea began to fidget and mutter, looking at her watch and rattling her program. Then she went into the act she had first imagined with Cady on the day of the great brainstorm. She played a woman who had apparently come to the wrong theater, who thought she was at a male strip show. Her embarrassed friend kept trying to shush her, but that only added fuel to her fire.

Augie Blake's discomfort was very real: he at first obviously believed that there was a real kook in the audience, and after a momentary hesitation, he gamely carried on. But as Thea got louder and louder, her voice must have given her away. He was stunned, but by that time Thea had taken over. Jumping out of her seat, she rushed onstage to undress him herself, and Augie Blake's look of horror wasn't faked. He was being made a fool of. It was one thing to be naked onstage, quite another to have a demented Thea, screaming "Lemme see it, I paid for a good look," tear off your clothes and attempt to examine your masculinity with a critical eye. It was obvious to all that Thea would go as far as Augie Blake let her.

If he had kept his presence of mind, he just might have made a recovery and somehow saved his scene, but that was asking a lot from any actor. Augie fought off Thea's hands as best he could, but when, after much shrieked encouragement, her fellow actress joined her, he fled the stage amid howls of audience laughter.

It would not have been overwhelmingly funny, except for Thea's marvelously drawn single-minded determination to get her money's worth. But Thea could be funny onstage just being Thea, and she had the knack of making an audience like her. What's more, the audience had been "stacked" with several other actors, friends of the cast, who had reason to want Augie Blake to get his comeuppance. Their delighted shrieks of laughter at Augie's discomfort had encouraged the rest of the audience, had set them laughing too.

From then on it was a rout. Augie could not do anything right. There came the moment, onstage, when he realized that the entire cast was in on it, and if Cady hadn't known so well how much he deserved this, she might have felt sorry for him. But there wasn't much the cast was doing to him that he hadn't done to one or the other of them during the past three months, and she had steeled her heart and enjoyed the ruthlessness of the lesson he was getting.

Afterward, the excitement was heady. The cast and

Cady and the half dozen other actors and actresses who had been sprinkled through the audience went off to a late-night restaurant and laughed and congratulated all concerned over food and drink.

Cady laughed as much as any of them, but inside she knew that her good humor was forced. In the midst of friends and companions, she felt more cut off than ever. She was an outsider. No matter how much her friends accepted and liked her, there was a voice inside that told her she did not belong.

There had always been a voice inside her telling her she did not belong, Cady realized suddenly. The only time she had ever truly felt she belonged had been... with Luke. With Luke she had let down her guard. She had let herself feel loved and believe she was loved. She had let herself love him.

Suddenly she had a racking headache, a thud-thud-thudding behind her eyes that made the lights painful and every shriek of laughter torture. Cady leaned across her neighbor and tapped Thea on the arm.

"I'm leaving now, okay?" she said softly. "Will you be home tonight?"

"Yes—no—I don't know," said Thea. "Depends how long I hang around here. Are you okay? Do you want me to come with you?"

"No." Cady smiled. "I'm fine, I just want to get home to bed. See you," she said to the table in general as she got to her feet. "Super show," she said, for the benefit of the cast. "Glad I was there to see it."

"Hey, Cady," said the actor sitting beside her, a man she had met for the first time tonight. "Going already? Say listen, can I call you?"

Oh, hell. She didn't know how to answer that. Why did men persist in asking you things like that in public? She couldn't say no, yet she didn't want to encourage him in the least. She didn't want even to talk to anyone who had a sexual interest in her. "Yeah, sure," she told him easily. "I'm staying with Thea." She would have to deal with him later, that meant, if he didn't change his mind or forget to phone. Hoping he would do just that, Cady slipped on her coat, waved a general goodbye and made her escape.

The restaurant was a two-part construction, the cheaper snacks and drinks in the back room, a more elegant dining area in front. Cady pulled her woolly hat down over her hair as she walked through the dining lounge, intent on her thoughts, not looking around. The voice came as a complete surprise.

"*Cady!*" he shouted loudly enough for the diners at several tables to turn and look at the same time as Cady did. "My God, Cady, it's you!"

Luke Southam was on his feet, his napkin forgotten in his hand, staring across the room at her. Cady stopped stock-still in amazement, and for a moment they were frozen there, mouths open, eyes wide with disbelief, in a tableau so theatrical it could have been arranged. The other patrons of the restaurant were entranced into silence, forks halfway to mouths, wine glasses arrested midair. But neither Cady nor Luke was even peripherally aware of anyone else.

Luke came to his senses first, throwing down his napkin and starting toward her across the room, and with that movement Cady's brain kicked into action and she turned and blindly headed for the door.

She had to get away. She couldn't face him again, mustn't let him know what he had done to her. What he might still have the power to do to her.... For in that first shocked moment it hadn't been the pain she had remembered—that had followed nearly instantly, but it hadn't been her first response. In that blinding, treacherous moment the thought that had raced through her mind had been the same one she had known that

first afternoon in Algonquin Park: *you made it*. And she
had felt the same flash of recognition.

She was as vulnerable to Luke right now as if she had
never made the hundred hard decisions she had made
these past days and nights; as easy a prey as if he had
never hurt her. Yet at the same time her heart was
strangling her with the pain of his betrayal, so that
breathing was impossible.

So she ran.

Luke heard the fascinated babble rise from the tables
around him at this rather unexpected turn of events, but
he was beyond caring.

"Cady!" he called after her. "Cady, wait!" People
shuffled their chairs aside for him with impossible slow-
ness, and he didn't know how he refrained from throwing them all bodily out of his way, but at last he was out
on the pavement. A jacketed, blue-jeaned figure was
running pell-mell down the street ahead of him, and
Luke set out after her, swiftly, silently, not wasting his
breath on calling her.

Dammit, she could run like a rabbit. And it was freezing out and he was in his shirt-sleeves. Any other
woman, he felt sure, would have collapsed after a couple of minutes at this pace; just his luck to fall in love
with one who had wings on her heels.

And no sense in her damned head. Why was she running away, anyway? He'd been searching heaven and
earth to find the woman for as far back as he could remember, had lucked out when he least expected it, and
here she was, running! It didn't make sense!

She was slowing down at last, and without looking
back. She hadn't looked back from the beginning, and
he wondered if she knew he was behind her, or if she'd
simply been running blind, running away from her
memories.

She stopped and turned and was waiting for him.

"What do you want?" she asked him coldly, her breathing quick but not labored.

Luke was panting. "Dammit," he heaved, "did I miss a mental turn or something? Why are you running away from me?"

"Why are you chasing me?" she countered.

"*Why?*" Luke breathed on his hands and mentally cursed the weather; it had no right to be so cold at the end of October! "Cady, for hell's sake, I've been looking for you high and low! I don't have your number, or your name, or— Why am I chasing you? Don't you *know* why?"

She looked at him blankly and shrugged. "I guess so," she said. *Because I ran away,* she was thinking stupidly. *What difference does it make, anyway? Like the old joke—you are here because of me and I am here because of you.*

"You guess so," Luke repeated. "You had my name, Cady, why didn't you— Look, I'm about to become an iceberg here. Could we get a taxi?" He shepherded her to the curb and flagged a passing cab. It was a good thing she had run toward Yonge Street and the heart of the city and not into the small back streets where taxis seldom cruised.

He gave the driver his address and turned toward her.

"Cady," he whispered. "Cady, Cady, Cady," as though he was incapable of saying anything else. "Come here." He pulled her against his chest, and she felt his cold skin against her cheek.

"You're freezing!" she accused him. "Luke, where's your coat?"

"With my dinner," he said, grinning. "Never mind that—you'll warm me. You're so warm, kiss me, Cady."

His lips were cold but gentle against hers, and she felt her heart quiver at his touch, as though it would have unfolded for him again. *I could be as vulnerable as ever,* she thought in surprise. *I must be a glutton for punishment.*

She let him kiss her, she kissed him back, she even enjoyed the smoky wine that curled against all her nerve ends, seducing her into languor. But she kept an ice padlock on her heart.

"My God," said Luke breathlessly in her ear. "Cady, I've needed you. I need you so much and it's been so long...." His hand stroked her denim-encased thigh, her arm through the thick stuff of her bomber jacket. "Cady—kiss me, Cady, kiss me, touch me—"

"Here we are!" announced the driver, stopping the cab with a small jerk. Then he turned and lifted his elbow over the back seat before they had quite recovered, taking a good look at them. "Not a moment too soon, eh?" he said suggestively, winking at Cady in a way that made her flesh crawl.

Luke felt the rage flare in his gut. "My wife doesn't like it when men look at her," he said in a tone of cold menace, and had the satisfaction of seeing the taxi driver's head snap around to the front. Luke dropped some bills on the seat beside him.

Outside on the pavement he looked at her ruefully. "Sorry," he said. "It was male chauvinist. But I couldn't stand that look on his face—I wanted to smash him. I'm sorry I let you in for it in the first place."

Cady giggled. "I'm no expert on what's chauvinist and what isn't," she told him. "But I was awful glad you put him in his place. I couldn't do it."

"No?" Luke looked surprised. One arm around her, he led her up the front path of a small house in a row of terraced houses.

"When a man like that decides a woman is a slut," she told him, "nothing she can say is going to change his mind. The more violent or rude she is, the more she confirms him in his opinion. No matter what she does, she is going to go away with the memory of his contempt somewhere in her brain. I don't know if that's chauvinist, either, but that's the kind of attitude I hate. I hate anybody who won't let me live the way I want to live, anyone who judges me by a whole lot of stupid rules I've never had time for anyway." She paused. "If he needed you telling him I'm a decent married woman to help him learn that every human being deserves respect, then I'm glad you told him."

Luke looked down at her, silently taking in her words as he dug keys out of his pocket. Cady shut herself up. She was talking too much. It was so easy to talk to Luke.

At one end of the terrace the houses looked dilapidated and neglected even by moonlight. At this end they had been reclaimed and renovated into very smart town houses. The door Luke was unlocking was of beautiful old polished oak, set into a wall of sandblasted pink brick.

"It's beautiful," Cady said, looking around. "I had no idea these houses were here. It's just like England." Terracing was much more common in England than in Canada, though perhaps modern town houses were a form of terracing. But these were almost like a mews, tiny and perfect.

As the door opened Cady breathed in a gasp of admiration. The smooth plastered walls were painted in the palest off-white, the floors and woodwork had all been sanded back to the original glowing wood and gleamed with varnish. One entire wall was the same pink brick as the outside, and everything looked comfortable and warm.

Luke led her up an open staircase to the second floor. Here the entire floor was one large room. At the front, beside a huge window that extended up into a skylight, was a desk surrounded by shelves of books and filing cabinets. The other end, entirely closed in by brick except for a huge skylight above the bed, served as his bedroom.

"It really is beautiful, Luke," she said. "Did you do it?"

He was beside her, taking her jacket off. He kissed her nose. "Yes," he said lightly. "Do you want a drink?"

Cady shook her head, and then she looked slowly around. "Luke," she said, "we're in your bedroom already."

He was hanging the jacket over a chair, and he turned his head and looked at her for a long moment. "So we are," he said at last, straightening. "Do you want to go downstairs?"

If it was a question of talking or making love, she could far more easily handle the lovemaking. Talking would only confuse her, perhaps destroy the careful barriers she had in place around her emotions. She needed Luke's lovemaking, she knew that much. It was a first—she couldn't remember ever having needed a man before—but still she could handle it. Emotions were different.

Cady shook her head. "No," she said clearly. "I'm happy where I am."

Luke crossed to her and kissed her, a long, slow, lingering kiss. By the time he lifted his head they were both breathing shakily. Luke's hands clasped her arms above the elbows then, and stood away from her. "First things first," he said, "before I forget."

He walked over to the study half of the floor, pulled out a crisp white notepad and set it on his desk in front of her, handing her a pencil.

"Put a telephone number where I can reach you, just in case I lose you again," he commanded. "I'm not taking any more chances."

Somehow in that moment it seemed all right. Cady

picked up the pencil and wrote down Thea's number, then smiled as he turned her to face him. He heaved a huge sigh of relief.

"I have nearly been out of my mind without you," he told her simply. "I never want to go through that again."

He kissed her hard, letting the pressure of his lips explain his anguish to her, and she didn't fight the fire that his knowing mouth set aflame in the pit of her stomach. She fought the tenderness that tugged at her heart, but she did not impede desire as it tingled delicately along her skin in the wake of his hands and lips.

Luke led her to the bed then, and pulled off the black turtleneck sweater she wore, and gasped in surprise as her full perfect breasts swelled into view. He swore softly.

"The sight of your breasts does more to me," he told her almost grimly, "than any other woman's mouth on me." He pulled her suddenly against him and pushed back her thick hair to kiss her neck, her throat and finally, her breasts. His hand found her nipple then, and he stroked and teased it and at the same time watched the expression on her face with a deep hunger in his eyes that took her breath away. She felt her own nipple grow into a bead under his touch, felt the touch of his strong fingers on her breast draw a response from deep in her womb, as though he strummed invisible cords that connected all the parts of her body to her center.

Cady sighed her desire and strained up to his lips, closing her eyes against the look in his.

When she undressed him there were red marks still on his left arm, and she looked away, not to be destroyed with the thought of perfect union that that time would remind her of.

This was not perfect union. She knew better than to let herself feel that again. This was a purely sexual union, demanded by their bodies, but not by their hearts. She would not have sought him out for it; away from his presence she would never have recognized that she felt it. But she did feel it, she wanted him, and as long as she kept her heart out of it, she was safe, just this once.

But once only. It was a strain to keep her heart out of it. Her heart wanted to call to him and be answered; her heart wanted to interpret the deep touch of his body in her as a message of love; her heart wanted to cry and cry for the joy of having found him again.

But her heart was kept in rigid silence. It was her body that cried out its joy at his nearness, that responded to his touch, that drowned in his passion. It was her body alone that was swayed by the rhythm, and rode the crescendo, and strained after completion and found it; and then rode the gentle spirals of its dying away down to earth again.

When her ears could hear again she heard him whispering meaningless love messages into her ear, and her body allowed him to draw her into his hold, settle her comfortably against his shoulder. Her body felt his kiss on her head but she ruthlessly quashed her heart's tender leap at the touch.

"Cady," Luke said, the thread of fulfillment thick in his voice. "We have to talk, Cady, but not now. Do you mind if we don't talk now?"

"No," she said.

"I love you," he said softly. She wondered if he noticed that she made no answer.

Luke stroked her gently and kissed her from time to time, and when the stroking stopped she knew he was asleep. She waited fifteen minutes, till his breath slowed and deepened, and then very gently she eased out of his hold, out of his warm bed into her familiar, safe, empty world. Silently as a cat she dressed; as silently crept to his desk and tore the top five pages from his notebook.

Downstairs she used the bathroom. On a sudden impulse, combing her hair, she slid open the mirrored door of the cabinet.

A bottle of Chanel No. 5, a tube of lipstick, two emery boards and a number of strictly feminine odds and ends were neatly grouped on the middle shelf. With a satiric grin Cady closed the cabinet, switched off the light, and crept out of the house and out of Luke's life.

The terraced houses weren't far from Yonge Street. She stood in the biting damp cold less than five minutes before a taxi stopped.

Cady sank into the back seat and closed her eyes. Immediately her body summoned up the memory of Luke's touch, the scent and shape of his body against hers.

Well, she thought, *that wasn't so bad. I've come out of it unscathed, so I've learned something. Anyway, it's good practice. All body and no heart, that's the trick. That's the way to do it. That's exactly how I've got to do it with Miles Davidson.*

CADY SLUMPED IN BOREDOM and rubbed her aching spine, wishing the high stool she was sitting on had some sort of back support.

"That flood still isn't bouncing right," someone shouted. "Can you angle it again, *please*?"

A makeup girl darted in through all the milling bodies and began to pat powder over Cady's face, destroying the fine sheen of sweat on her brow and upper lip.

"Could we get going again, please?" a petulant voice demanded. "Could you clear the set, please?"

"Clear the set, please! Clear the set!"

"Wait a minute, wait a minute," demanded a man who had been unrolling the cord of his hair dryer along the floor as he approached Cady. "She's got some wet tendrils!"

No one laughed except Cady, though the self-important exasperation in his tone could have betokened a far greater disaster—like the sky falling in. She straightened her back as the hairdresser, who had pinned her hair up at least a dozen times already, delicately and expertly dried her tendrils of sweat-dampened hair against his hand.

At her breast she felt a twitching and switched her gaze to the person who was perfecting the already perfect fall of the lace camisole against her skin.

"All right, we're rolling! Okay, Katie, ready...action...small turn of the head, that's it, perfect...your lips, relax your lips, aaand...right hand up, now the left, good, good...."

"Cut!" With a small sigh Cady relaxed and dropped her arms.

"Her lips are flat, Susan. Can we get some more gloss on her lips? We're not picking that up."

After an age, they were rolling again. Cady's arms were aching with the length of time she had sat holding her hands to her hair today.

"Action, Katie...head around, that's it, lovely...your lips are right, that's right, you're looking very kissable, he'll notice any moment...that's it, that's it...right hand up, left hand...up...that's it, and...one pin comes out...and down, that's great, that's perfect, and another pin...that's it, and a little half-smile and a look across, that's it, you've got him now, right, and the last pin, and it's all tumbling down, jeez, perfect, that's perfect, and now you shake it loose, gently, very gently, that's perfect, Katie, and now you look over at him, a little knowing look, thaaat's it, a little smile...*cut*.

"Perfect, Katie, that was perfect." The director raised his voice. "That okay with everyone?"

There was no dissent, but still she sat there for ten minutes, the hairdresser hovering beside her, calling at random moments to no one in particular, "Do I put this up again? Are we doing another take?"

At last a male voice called out, "Okay, that looks like a wrap! Thank you very much, Katie. Thanks, everyone!" and she stood up and followed the makeup girl back to the makeup room to have it all taken off by expert fingers.

It was five to five by the time she got out in the street again. She had been in the studio nearly ten hours. Well, she felt it. Every minute of that incredibly boring session had dragged by. All the milling around, all the waiting, all the elaborate setting up, only to have someone call "cut" ten seconds after the camera got rolling. And every time her hair had had to be put up perfectly, held up by one pin, two others set in without carrying the weight of more than a few tendrils.

She had read the one-page shooting script, though she had no lines. In the final film there would be her face, facing the camera, head up. A man's voice, a voice-over, would be talking business, like a tired husband after a long day. And then Cady would tilt her head and start to pull pins out of her hair, and the voice would falter and die. When her hair came cascading down the voice would say softly, "Hey...I missed you," and Cady would smile her slow smile. Then the shampoo would flash on the screen and a woman's voice would whisper the name like a secret to the millions of watching women.

A bit different from the usual shampoo commercial, where one or another female star swore she'd never used anything else since the day she was born. And it was pretty good money for a day's work. Her agent had demanded well above scale, and they had paid it. Nothing like what a star would get, but good rent-paying money. And if it aired longer than the standard thirteen weeks, she'd get a nice little check every now and again.

Or if it was deemed successful there might be a series of similar ads.... Though whether they would want the same face each time, or a lot of different faces, was anyone's guess. In the meantime, Cady could scratch "shampoo" off her list. She would not be able to advertise another brand of shampoo for several years.

Her appointment with George Talousien was scheduled for five-fifteen, and if the traffic would let up a little bit, she would just make it. Cady found a parking space for Thea's little blue car just a few yards down from the Equity office and, clutching her portfolio case, dashed up the steps and through the door at five-sixteen.

The secretary behind the desk eyed her blankly. "Kate Hunter," Cady said. "To see George Talousien."

"George Talousien!" exclaimed the girl. "Oh, you've missed him. He was here ages ago—must be weeks ago now."

Cady laughed in relief. For a moment she had thought George had cast the part with someone else and left without telling her. "Yes, but he's back, isn't he?" She smiled. "I have an appointment for today, now."

The secretary shook her head mysteriously. "If he is, he hasn't told us."

"Can I use your phone?" Cady asked, and at her nod picked up the receiver and dialed Pat's office.

"Where am I supposed to be meeting George Talousien?" she demanded without preamble.

"Oh, hell!" Pat said instantly. "Did I forget to tell you? Are you at Equity?"

"Yes, and yes."

"Oh, hell, Katie, he's over at Sutton Place. Oh, hell, I'm sorry. Look, grab a cab straight over there and I'll call and explain to him. Hell, he's got to catch a plane tonight, I don't know what time, either. Just get over there fast, okay? Room 1606."

Cady slammed down the phone and dashed out, but crosstown traffic was heavy and it was twenty to six before she pulled up at the front door of the Sutton Place hotel. As she dashed into the lobby she recognized George Talousien heading for the doors, a small suitcase in his hand. She walked up to him.

"Hi!" she smiled. "Sorry I'm late! I guess it's too late to talk to you."

"Katie," he greeted her. "Yes, what a pity. I really wanted to talk to you. I'd really— Look, could you come to the airport with me, just come along in the cab? We would talk on the way."

"Listen, I've got a car. I'll drive you," said Cady, marveling at how much trouble she was taking to get a job offer she intended to turn down.

THEA WAS SHAKING HER HEAD and laughing. "Only George could dream that one up," she was saying. "Lady Macbeth as one of the witches!" She covered her eyes. "Do I believe what I'm hearing? A seminude Lady Macbeth prancing around a caldron and inciting her husband to regicide?" She laughed again. "Did he say whether it's a witch taking on her image to tempt him, or whether Lady Mac really has sold her soul to the devil?"

Cady looked at her. "He didn't say, but what difference does it make? You'd never be able to make it clear to the audience."

"Oh, I don't know, he might have her dusting off her broom when the letter arrives."

"So he could," said Cady faintly. "Heaven forbid."

"Listen, the critics will say it's brilliant, especially if they get enough breast and leg in the caldron scene," Thea said. "Still, I'm glad it won't be you. Regina in winter *and* Lady Macbeth as succubus—it would be too much."

Cady didn't answer. She was almost certain of getting the part—George Talousien hadn't disguised the fact that he had thought he saw his Lady Mac in her, and that seeing her again had pretty well convinced him. When the phone rang early that afternoon and Pat's voice announced that the part was hers, she was not surprised.

"He wants an answer this afternoon, if you can decide," Pat told her. "What do you think, Katie?"

"I'll call you back in ten minutes."

Thea's ears had picked up. "You didn't tell him no?"

"No," agreed Cady.

"Why not? What are you going to do?"

Cady picked the phone up and with trembling fingers dialed a number. "I'm calling Miles Davidson," she said. "Something's happened. Something's gone wrong, or he would have called me. I want to know what."

"Miles?" she said when she got through, not surprised to find that he was in town, but wondering how long he had been here without letting her know. "It's Cad—Kate Hunter. How are you?"

"Katie!" his voice exclaimed, very friendly. "Hey—I was going to call you."

Her heart sank only momentarily, and then she recovered. "Well, I've saved you the trouble. Look, Miles, I've had a job offer that might conflict a bit with the tentative schedule you mentioned to me, and I was wondering. . . ."

She broke off and her hand tightened on the receiver. Thea leaned forward, praying a little, straining for any clue of what the man might be saying. At long last Cady said goodbye, hung up the phone and turned to her friend.

"His financing has fallen through," she told Thea in a surprised voice. The disappointment hadn't hit her yet. "He's lost some of his backers. Everything's at a standstill till he finds new backers. He's leaving town again tomorrow. Everything's at a standstill now till Christmas at least.''

Thea sucked in a breath and shook her head sympathetically. This was almost worse than losing the part to another actress. Because you'd have to be a fool not to know that this might change everything. After Christmas, with new backers, Miles Davidson might be starting up a whole new project. He might have a new screenplay that cut some of the characters out. He might have a whole new story. He might have an entirely different star in mind, one who would require the rethinking of all the other parts.

"Gee, I'm sorry, Cady. I'm really sorry."

"So am I," said Cady. "But I'm not going to sit around and mope. I'm not sitting around this town all winter regretting things. I'm getting sick of this town."

Strangely, through the crushing disappointment, she felt the faintest thread of relief. She could get out of town, she could get away from the threat of Luke finding her, bumping into her, making her life a misery. At least she could do that. "You know what I'm going to do? I'm going to go to Regina and play Lady Macbeth as succubus."

Running away again, she thought distantly. *That's what Luke called it, and I guess that's what I'm best at.*

And yet there was no escaping the fact that Regina was in her home province, and that it was the city she had spent most of her childhood in. This would be the first time she had been back in ten years. Maybe it wasn't as bad as it seemed.

Was she running from, or running to?

7

Hank Southam scratched his head, cleared his throat and looked uncomfortable. "Uh, pity about you and Sharon," he said, for perhaps the tenth time. His knee was bobbing up and down, a typical nervous movement.

Luke's eyelids drooped and his face took on a bored look. "Hmm," he grunted noncommittally.

Hank tried again. "The girls really miss her." He nodded, agreeing with himself. "They miss her a lot."

"The girls" referred to Hank's wife, Darlene, and his and Luke's sister, Leah. The three couples usually spent a lot of time together, and Luke could understand their disappointment. But if they thought he was going to choose a wife by means of a family poll, they'd better think again.

He shrugged in faint anger. "Well, then, why don't they see her? I don't care."

"Yeah. They, ah . . . well, as a matter of fact, Luke, uh, they—they have seen her. Darlene has, for sure." For a faint moment Hank wished that she had not. "Leave Luke to himself," he had warned his wife. "He won't thank you for interfering." But Sharon professed herself unhappy at the split, and everybody could see that Luke was nearly desperate with misery. Darlene had snorted, "Oh, you men! You can't see what's under your nose! He's *miserable*, Hank, and we've got to do something!"

For we *read* you, Hank was now thinking dryly. But

Darlene wasn't an interfering person, she simply cared a lot. And when he looked, of course it was obvious that Luke had made a mess of something.

So Hank took a deep breath and hoped his wife was right and that his brother would thank him in the end. "As a matter of fact," he said, in as casual a voice as he could muster, "Sharon's pretty miserable about it all, Luke. She— Hell, Luke, I don't want to interfere!" he burst out suddenly, ignoring his wife's injunction to go slowly. "But Sharon's still in love with you, still wants to marry you. She'd like to give it another try, if you would. So if there's anything a go-between can do to sort things out— Well, we just want you to know that everything's possible, if you know what I mean."

Luke put a hand to his eyes and stared down into his drink. The chatter of women's voices in the kitchen had stopped momentarily, and he knew that Darlene and Leah were casting telling looks at each other.

"Look, Hank," he began helplessly, rubbing his forehead. Suddenly he felt as far from his family as from Mars. "I don't—" Hell, how could he explain it? "I don't want to marry Sharon. I don't love her enough. I thought maybe I might, but I don't."

"Okay," said Hank. "You won't change your mind, eh?"

"No, I won't change my mind. Tell Darlene...not to encourage her, please. She comes around to see me enough as it is—she keeps dropping in once a week to pick up something else she's left behind." He was briefly angry. Sharon knew there was no hope of him changing his mind. The only thing she could be hoping for now was that public opinion—pressure from his family— could force him into a relationship or a marriage he didn't want. Suddenly he wondered if Sharon had felt anything more for him in their comfortable relationship than just the desire for a comfortable husband.

Hank laughed. "Women!" he said. "Well, then, if it isn't woman trouble that's got you looking like a death's-head, what is it?"

Luke grinned ruefully at him. "Woman trouble," he said.

Hank looked momentarily stunned, and then he made a silent amused "oh" of understanding and glanced toward the kitchen in half-laughing alarm. "Oh, boy!" he said. "Complications, huh?"

"Complications," agreed Luke.

"Are you going to bring her around?" Hank asked tentatively.

"Yes, I'm going to bring her around," Luke told him without heat. "I'm going to marry her—when I find her," he added thoughtfully.

THE FINDING PART wasn't going very well. In fact he had about come to a dead end. After going through the drawers of Dee's filing cabinet, an unholy task that made him glad his brief sojourn in Hollywood had been unsuccessful, there hadn't seemed much else he could do. Briefly he toyed with the idea of flying to Saskatchewan to look through all the births recorded during the five or ten years when she must have been born. But even if births were available by year, and even assuming she was the only baby named Caedmon during that period, what would he gain? Her birth name, which, given her checkered childhood history and her adult profession, she might have abandoned years ago.

For the life of him he could not understand why she didn't appear in the usual records of actors. Even if she used another name professionally, surely he would have recognized her photo? Luke woke up nights tortured by a dream that he had somehow missed her photo in Dee's files—that it had been stuck to the back of another, or so arty, as some of them had been, that her face was basically unrecognizable.

He had attended every play, revue, showcase and even poetry reading in Toronto during the past month, hoping to find her onstage. He had even sat through an appallingly written play called *The Mirror* at the Royal Alex in which an actor had sat and talked to his reflection for two hours—and had also spoken *for* his reflection. After the first half hour it was blatantly obvious that this was a one-man show, but Luke had sat through it all, just in case. It was possible—his writer's instinct told him that this was nongenre, or even antigenre writing, in which no trick was too low for the writer to play on the audience—it was distantly possible that in the last minute of the play the woman the man kept talking about might materialize, or some such rubbish. An actress, for greater impact, given no forewarning credit on the programme. . . .

But it didn't happen. All that happened was that the monologue came to an end and the young actor, who must have been astonishingly brilliant to have given the thing any kind of integrity at all, stood at the front of the stage and accepted far less applause than was his due. On his way out Luke saw the sign across the actor's photo: "A one-man tour de force!" *Toronto Star*, and sighed. He could have saved himself the trouble.

He could have saved himself the trouble of watching television, too, it seemed. No matter how much appallingly written, badly acted "Canadian content" he watched, he had to be satisfied with virtue as its own reward. Cady never appeared, even as an extra.

Of that he was certain. He had rented a video recorder, and he watched the programmes with it constantly ready. With the push of a remote button, Luke could instantly record any crowd scene for later play-back and, if necessary, minute examination at the slowest speed.

If she was a television actress, nothing she had done

appeared in any original programming on any Canadian channel.

He was almost relieved for her. Much of what he had so painstakingly watched had been second-rate. Luke began to think fondly of his short stint in Hollywood and the screenplay he had written for Dee. Except for the surroundings—he had hated Hollywood— Luke had enjoyed doing what was required of him. He had been right to leave Hollywood, but perhaps he shouldn't have let the experience sour him on screenwriting.

When I find Cady, he thought, *I'll write screenplays for her.*

In the meantime, what he was writing for her was very different, and much simpler: he took out ads in the personal columns of the *Star* and the *Globe,* ads that read simply, "Cady, please call." But she did not call, nor did she answer by means of another ad.

He had watched her write down her phone number that night, and now he cursed himself for not taking it before she had changed her mind. But at least he remembered the first three digits of that number, and he knew it was a Cabbagetown exchange. He had spent a lot of days and evenings driving around Cabbagetown streets, hoping for a glimpse of her. It was a long shot, but long shots weren't to be despised when that was all you had.

Sometimes he tried to understand why she was running, what could let her make love to him one hour and run off without leaving any trace the next. He didn't believe she didn't love him. It would be a cold day in hell before he would make himself believe that. She was going to have to tell him to his face—tell him long and hard—before he would believe that. And before she could do that, he was going to have to find her.

GEORGE TALOUSIEN MET HER at the airport during a blizzard. It was Halloween afternoon, but Cady couldn't imagine there would be many ghosts and witches abroad tonight.

"What a welcome home!" she exclaimed, laughing after they had fought their way through the driving snow and at last gained the car.

"Oh yes," he said, "you're a native of these parts, aren't you?"

Cady was grinning broadly. There was something about the snow that thrilled her, as though she had scented a challenge and her blood was up. "I sure am," she agreed.

"How does it feel to be coming home?"

She laughed again. "Good," she admitted. "It feels real good. I shouldn't have stayed away so long."

"How long?"

"Ten years."

"Do you have a lot of people here?" George asked. By people she knew he meant family, but sometimes you had to take family where you found it.

"Yes," she agreed, "I have a lot of people here. Spread around some—it's going to be a trick getting to see everybody."

The trick was going to be finding them at all. It had been twenty-one years since her grandparents had been killed and she had left Sturgis, and her friend Shirley might have left Sturgis—even Saskatchewan—long ago. Cady did not intend to look up the long string of foster parents she had lived with afterward, though she would like to drive around those old neighborhoods if she could find them.

The neighborhoods where she had lived with the Simpsons would be easy to find, and friends from those days would be easy to track down. Some of them she had last seen only nine or ten years ago, when she had graduated from high school and packed her bags and gone east to the big city and theater school.

She had been so full of purpose then, going off into the world to become a famous actress. She had felt something like a sense of mission, to become someone.

She was surprised now to feel another, quieter sense of mission overtake her, as though it had been lying in her undiscovered for a long time. Now, Cady realized, as the half-familiar streets of Regina, covered in white and blurred by the blowing snow, moved past the car windows, her purpose was to find herself.

"Jenny lives close to the rehearsal hall," George Talousien was saying as Cady surfaced with a start, "so you'll be pretty much within walking distance of both the hall and the theater. If this weather keeps up that'll be a boon."

She had agreed to share an apartment with the actress playing Lady Macduff, who had been living in Regina for some time and formed a part of what seemed to be a semipermanent company of actors here. George stopped the car in front of a large prewar brick house with an enormous open veranda running around two sides of the ground floor. Cady drew in a breath. It was the sort of house that had always meant solidity and security to her, the sort of place that had always seemed to house large, happy families, that had always emphasized her isolation.

"Here?" she asked doubtfully.

"Right here," agreed George cheerfully, reaching to unlock the back door of the car. "Jenny should be here to meet you."

They pulled her luggage from the back seat, where they had put it because the banged-up old car, as George had told her, had a temperamental trunk lock that wouldn't open in cold weather.

The whirling snow blew into her eyes and down her

turned-up collar as George and Cady struggled to lift her luggage over the giant snowbank at the curb formed by the snowplowing of the streets. For Cady it was more and more like coming home. Never in England and rarely in Toronto had she seen snow like this.

As they got to the bottom of the wide, gray-painted veranda steps, a small blond woman opened the big front door of the house and called something that was lost on the wind. Cady staggered up the steps with one case as George followed with two, and fell gratefully into the small protection the veranda roof afforded her with a deep breath of relief. The blond woman darted out and grabbed the case from her hand. "Come on!" she shouted into Cady's ear against the wind. "You're going to freeze!"

Cady didn't realize how noisy the storm was till the front door was shut and she felt the silence of the big house all around her. "Boy!" she exclaimed, stamping the snow from her boots and shaking off her woolly tam. "That's some weather."

"You're lucky you landed when you did," the woman told her. "They're going to close the airports. Mrs. Manning says it's going to be like the Great Blizzard of 1955."

Cady laughed aloud. "Oh, no! Thea *said* I'd get snowed in till spring!"

"Cady, Jenny," George introduced them. "Can I leave you two girls? I'd like to get home while I can."

"Sure," they said in unison, and he wrapped his scarf a little more securely around his neck and turned to the door.

"See you both in the morning," he said. He had told Cady that there was a company call for first read-through at 10:00 A.M.

"If you get there," Jenny said, grinning.

When he was gone she turned to Cady and smiled.

"Let's get this stuff upstairs and get you settled," she said. "I'll show you around."

When they had wrestled the luggage up the dark walnut staircase to the second floor, she led Cady around the upstairs landing to a room at the front of the house. "We're not really sharing," she explained. "Mrs. Manning rents out rooms to the company. We have the two best rooms—we both face front. I'm in the one just across the hall from you."

The room was large, with a wide window overlooking the veranda roof and the street. "In the summer we crawl out the window and sunbathe out there, though Mrs. Manning doesn't like it. She thinks it's too dangerous."

It looked dangerous. The roof was sloping and shingled, and it looked to Cady as though you'd have to brace your feet against the eavestroughing. But she wouldn't have to worry about sunbathing: the snow was thick out there.

There was a desk, a big walk-in closet, a large old-fashioned dresser and a double bed. There was a lot of walnut around, and it might have been somber except for the light floral wallpaper and the pretty curtains at the windows.

"This must have been the master bedroom," Cady said on a note of inquiry. It was a beautiful room.

"Yup," Jenny agreed. "You're wondering why you get it when you're the last to arrive, right? I'll tell you later." She led Cady down the hall toward the back of the house. "That's Tom's room at the top of the stairs. Tom's the stage manager, you'll like him. This—" Jenny turned right through another doorway to a room immediately behind Cady's "—is the communal sitting room. Mrs. Manning sometimes invites us downstairs, but she doesn't like us to hang out down there." There were chairs and a table in one corner, an old television set, and a couch and armchair. "We can bring our food up here to eat if we want to, or eat in the kitchen—she doesn't mind."

At the back of the house was an old-fashioned bathroom and beside it a small, narrow room with a sloping roof that housed a cot, a chair and a dresser. "Mrs. Manning has her own bathroom downstairs, and we share this one. She only rents out the little room if the theater has a problem with accommodation. She likes to keep it empty otherwise. Sometimes we can use it for an overnight guest or something, but if you do that you have to wash the sheets and put them back. The washer and dryer are in the basement. Are you hungry? I could show you the kitchen now, or later, whatever you like."

"Let's go now," said Cady. "I could use a cup of something."

There was a back staircase that led directly into the kitchen. A large gray-haired woman was standing at the sink, and Jenny introduced her as Mrs. Manning.

The woman looked a little worriedly at Cady. "I hope you'll like it here," she said, and Cady wondered why she sounded doubtful. "I hope you'll be happy."

"She'll be happy all right, Mrs. Manning," announced Jenny breezily. "Cady's the levelheaded type, I can tell." She turned to Cady. "You don't suffer from an overactive imagination, do you?"

"I don't think so," Cady replied, a little bemused by Jenny's rather determined bounciness. It did not suit her serene-blond image, but you couldn't help warming to her.

"There, I told you so!" she said gaily. "Here, let me show you the fridges. This one is Mrs. Manning's, and we're not supposed to—" she threw a grin toward the older woman "—to steal milk out of it when we run out. Are we, Mrs. Manning? If you're broke or you've run out of food, just do your best imitation of a starved cat

because she can't resist that, can you, Mrs. Manning?"
Jenny grinned again. "But don't steal the milk!" With
hardly a breath she went on, "Here's our fridge. Your
shelves are half the top shelf—the left-hand side of the
freezer—and the next one down. Mine are the right side
of the freezer and the second one down, and Tom has the
bottom shelf and the little shelf on the door. If you're
starved you can borrow from me, but please tell me
about it and put it back later. I don't advise you take anything from Tom's shelves, he hates that. He likes knowing where everything is and he remembers to a millimeter
how much butter he's got left, things like that." She
closed the fridge door. "You'll appreciate that at work—
Tom's a great S.M., there's never a prop out of place.
That's your cupboard there. I'll show you that when
we've gone shopping, okay? See you, Mrs. Manning!"

As they climbed the back staircase again Cady was
feeling a little as though she'd been caught up in a whirl-
wind. Jenny seemed to get more excitable as she went
on. "Oh!" she said suddenly, stopping dead in her tracks
so that Cady almost bumped into her on the narrow,
steep staircase. "You wanted something to drink! Look,
why don't you go and unpack, and I'll make you a cup
of cocoa, or coffee if you'd rather, okay?"

"Thanks," said Cady helplessly, feeling as though
she'd been well and truly taken in hand. "Thanks. Anything hot is just fine."

In her bedroom she sank down onto the bed with a
sigh and looked around. Well, it was not so different
from England, though in England she had progressed to
the point where she took self-contained flats when she
was out of town. If she had known she was coming to a
rooming house she might have told the theater that she
preferred the added expense of an apartment, but somehow she had got the impression that she would be sharing an apartment with Jenny.

Well, she didn't really regret this. She had decided in Toronto that she didn't want to live alone here. Her memories of Regina were pretty lonely ones for the most part. If she was making a pilgrimage to her past, or even if she was just running away from Luke, she needed company. She needed the strength of companionship. One way or another she had spent too much time alone. It was time to heal the wounds.

No ONE WAS LATE for rehearsal the next morning. The storm had died and the skies were bright as Cady and Jenny struggled along the Regina sidewalks through the night's mammoth accumulation of snow.

"This is nothing; everybody will make it in time," Jenny predicted as they stopped outside the single-story corrugated-steel building that housed The Old Foundry Theatre Company offices and rehearsal hall. "It used to be their playing space back in the seventies," she told Cady as they pulled open a huge steel door and walked through a deserted lobby and past an office or two to a large space beyond. "But when the new complex was built they moved into the theater there. George doesn't produce during the summer; another company takes over the theater then. It's a great rehearsal space, except when it rains—which isn't very often. When it does it rattles on that tin roof so hard we can't hear ourselves. It can get pretty funny."

There were three other people in the room, and Jenny introduced Cady to two of them, fellow actors playing Banquo and Malcolm. The third one, a dark, thickset, powerful-looking man, she apparently did not know, but Cady did.

"Nick!" she cried happily. "Nice to see you again!"

"Well, Cady Hunter," said Nick, smiling down at her. "Where have you been hiding yourself since theater school?" Nick had graduated in Cady's first semester.

They had never had a rehearsal or a class together, but in the theater-school world everyone had known everyone.

"I went to England," she told him, and they stood a moment exchanging brief histories. "What are you playing?" Cady asked at last.

"Macbeth," Nick responded. "And I guess you're my lady?"

Cady laughed. Nick was a strong actor; she would enjoy playing opposite him. "And a witch, of course," she agreed.

Nick's brows snapped together. "What?"

Cady's eyes twinkled. "You haven't heard? In a brilliant new interpretation George has decided that Lady Mac tempts Macbeth in two fronts—in the bedroom and by the caldron."

"You're playing one of the three sisters?" he repeated, startled.

"George thinks it's a great innovation, but I wonder if he's just trying to cut down on paychecks," Cady went on. "Jenny thinks she may be playing a witch, too. It's all right for her, but my costume change between Act III Scene IV and Act IV Scene I is going to be pretty innovative all on its own. Of course, he sees me as a half-naked witch, so perhaps I shouldn't call it a costume *change*, exactly." She laughed.

Nick was laughing, too, a deep throaty laugh, a sensuous admiring laugh that put Cady instantly on her guard. She could imagine that he used the laugh and his masculine good looks to great effect with women, and in college, if she remembered, he had cut a wide swath through the women of his year. "You're not playing the witch *as Lady Macbeth*?" he demanded in disbelief.

"Oh yes, I am," Cady contradicted him. "I told you George—"

She broke off because Jenny was beside her with

someone else to introduce, and a glance showed her that most, if not all, of the other actors had arrived. By the time she was introduced to everyone, George Talousien was in the room.

When the cast was settled on chairs in a large circle, George opened a looseleaf binder, his director's book, into which, on looseleaf paper, the pages of the play had been cut and pasted. He began to list everyone's names and the part or parts each actor would play. There was a short slim girl who would play both the third witch and Fleance, as well as other minor parts; Jenny would play the second witch and Cady the first. Several parts—Donalbain as well as one or two noblemen, Hecate and odd others—were cut completely, and George went through the play scene by scene, outlining the cuts he had made in the play. When this was over it was time for a coffee break, and during the general melee Cady approached the director.

She said, "I have a couple of very tight changes, George. I guess you know."

He looked at her over the rim of a Styrofoam cup. "You should be able to handle everything easily, Cady, except the end of Act III."

"The end of Act III is going to be quite a problem now that you've cut the two intervening scenes, George. It's straight from Lady Mac to the witches."

The director was unperturbed. "I've got a couple of ideas for that," he told her calmly. "It's possible to do the first half of the witches' scene there with just voices, and Macbeth in the middle of the stage; the witches won't come on till he speaks. That's one possibility."

Cady tried to imagine changing costume in the wings while she called lines from offstage. Faintly she asked, "What's the other idea?"

George took a sip of coffee. "Macbeth might exit from Scene IV alone," he mused, "and you could summon the other two witches to you. We could have wind and thunder and you could lose your costumes right on-stage—you know, traveling time and space. I think it would work.''

Cady looked at him, blinking. She did not think it would work, not at all. It would confuse one half of the audience and probably make the other half derisive. But her instinct told her not to oppose George Talousien, who according to Thea had a reputation for a fine madness and for not liking to be crossed. If she argued, he might carry out that idea for sheer bloody-mindedness. Any other director would have taken the interval at the end of Act III, in any case. It was the natural place for it.

But Cady only nodded coolly and asked, ''Would you mind if I had the second witch instead of the first?''

''Why?'' His brows came together.

Cady went warily. ''Well, the first witch is a longer part. Without Hecate she's definitely the head honcho, George.'' She grinned at him. She had been surprised to get anything but the second witch's part: if anything went amiss with a costume change she would be much less noticeable as the second. And besides, the first witch would have to carry most of the witches' scenes, and Cady could do without the additional pressure. She couldn't understand why George hadn't seen that and made allowances.

But George, it seemed, had not handed the numbers out at random. He *wanted* Cady to be the most visible witch. He wanted the audience to make the connection immediately.

''Oh,'' was all Cady said, her instinct again telling her not to push him.

Tom, the stage manager, was calling for an end to the coffee break, and everyone began to head back to their seats. Cady sank down next to Jenny again, and whispered, ''Have you worked with George a lot?''

Jenny had the lead in the play that had just opened at the theater and would run every night through the three weeks of Macbeth rehearsals. It was probably not politic to say anything unflattering about George, but Cady would dearly have loved to talk to someone. She hoped she hadn't signed on with a theatrical maniac.

"I've been here since August," Jenny told her. "He's done a play every six weeks on average. I've been in most of them. Why?"

Cady laughed lightly. "Oh, well, I'm a bit worried about this witch thing," she said. "I guess he knows what he's doing, does he?"

Jenny looked at her. "Well," she said matter-of-factly, "George's genius comes out in only two ways—stuff that is so fantastically innovative they call him a genius, and stuff that's so ridiculously offbeat it ends up being embarrassing to go onstage every night."

Cady's heart sank. "Oh great," she said faintly.

"The worst of it is," Jenny continued, "that you never know which you're in till opening night."

Cady stared at her in mingled astonishment and horror. "Are you serious?" she demanded.

"Oh yes," said Jenny. "Sometimes I wonder if it isn't just that in some ways the audiences haven't caught up with—"

"All right, Act I, Scene I," said Tom in a soft voice, but everyone immediately quieted. "Thunder and lightning. . . ."

Cady looked down at her open script, then up to where Nick faced her across the circle. He winked at her. Cady winked back, her eyes twinkling with amusement. It would be self-defeating to set herself up against her director, no matter how ridiculous his ideas seemed to her. The only way to get through this would be, as in any other production, to give it all she had. Regina was not, after all, the West End or Broadway, or even

Toronto. Experiment was good for the creative fires,
and where better to experiment with madness? She
wasn't judging George Talousien till all the votes were
in. Cady flicked her glance toward his disheveled,
saturine countenance.

". . .and begin," said Tom.

" 'When shall we three meet again,' " Cady asked, " 'in
thunder, lightning, or in rain?' "

THE HOUSE WAS STILL THERE. Number 105 Randolph
Street had hardly changed at all. The trees were taller,
but the neighborhood was the same: a quiet mixture of
old houses and new—or what had been new fifteen
years ago, Cady amended mentally. The Simpsons had
lived in an older house, a frame two story that had once
been painted white with red trim at windows and doors.
Now the trim was blue, but the paint was still reasonably fresh and the house had a cared-for look.

She had almost expected to find it gone, to find a
modern bungalow where the lilac and the big oak tree
had shaded the slightly shabby front porch. Perhaps
in the past ten years life had moved more slowly on
the prairies than elsewhere, but whatever had caused
this house to be left standing made her inordinately
grateful.

She stood on the sidewalk and gazed while the memories came and went in her. This was the only house, in
all her long years as a foster child, where she had felt
like one of the family. Houses had always been a special
source of pain to her, especially at night, when from the
outside they could look so welcoming, with light spilling out and warmth and laughter within. Cady sometimes felt she had spent her life on the outside of such
houses, on the outside, looking in.

Only this house had been different. In this house she
had belonged, like any ordinary young teenager. In this

house she had felt free to be herself, and she had blossomed.

In this house she had heard Bob Dylan for the first time, had pasted up posters of the Beatles. In this house she had sweated over the stove to tie-dye a T-shirt, had worn her first pair of false eyelashes, sewn a Ban the Bomb patch on the pocket of her bell-bottomed blue jeans.

In a little room upstairs over the back kitchen she had dressed for her first date with Donnie White, at the age of thirteen, taking as much care over her sneakers, jeans and jean jacket, Margery Simpson had laughed, as an earlier generation had taken with their strapless evening dresses. Her hair had been long and flowing even then, and that night for the first time she had braided two small braids beside her ears and left the rest loose, and she had thought with a new, female pride how grown-up she looked.

Cady sighed. The oak tree was naked now, its branches black against the snow, and she felt suddenly that her life was as barren as the tree. She stood still, hands deep in the pockets of her thick coat, and wondered why she felt so sad, looking at the house where she had been happy for the first time in years. How had she failed her thirteen-year-old self, so that what she felt now was her own disappointment?

Not through her career. Young Cady had wanted to be a success at something. She had even then wanted to "be somebody," though she hadn't chosen acting yet. A television reporter at one time, Cady remembered, a lawyer, prime minister—all her ideas had focused on the visible occupations. And now she was in a visible occupation and she was reasonably, and on the verge of being highly, successful at it. So that wasn't what disappointed her younger self, made her feel a sense of urgency, as though there was something she had not done and must do. Cady searched inside herself for the answer, realizing what a habit this sort of search had become in the past few...since Luke. That was when it had begun, when Luke had put her through the process of remembering, of searching, of trying to understand. And she had let him start the process in her, painful as it was, because she had known somehow that this sort of understanding was the road to freedom, the freedom from her own past.

Just like a psychiatrist, she thought cynically. Except that a shrink didn't get so involved with a patient that it killed her to leave him.

The thought of Luke brought to light the answer to her question: at thirteen she had still believed in happiness, and in love. She would have expected twenty-eight-year-old Cady to have loved deeply, to have a lover or a husband whom she loved and who loved her. In those brief, beautiful days of the Good Time, Cady had learned to trust again, and all her deep need for security had come to the surface. She had dreamed of staying here for years, in her little room over the back kitchen, of it being always her home to come back to. She had dreamed of marrying Donnie and going to live in a house just like it, and having children and an ordinary life. In those days the dream had been never to travel again, never to move....

But the adult Cady had shut herself off from love, from stability and security, and from trust. She expected no permanence except the sort of permanence that Thea gave her—of being unchanged, of being a fixed point in Cady's constantly moving life.

Moving in what direction? her young self demanded, *and toward what goal?* And she knew suddenly that the direction was "around in circles" and the goal was "away"—away from permanence or security or any threat of love. Only her career had any forward motion: her life itself had no direction at all.

"When you ain't got nuthin', you got nuthin' to lose...." It was in this house that she had first heard that song, but it wasn't till later that she had finally and utterly accepted it as the code she would live by.

Nothing to lose. But that meant that you were always losing, because everyday you had to let go of something that might come to be important to you.

As she had done all her life since she had left this house.

As she had done... with Luke.

REHEARSAL TIME WAS SHORT: they had only four weeks. And much of the last week would be taken up with technical and lighting rehearsals, and the problem of moving from the rehearsal space to the theater and the set, and dealing with costumes and props. For a play like Macbeth it was a very short time, as George pointed out to them.

"Everybody off the book by Monday, yes?" he admonished them late Friday afternoon after only four days of rehearsal.

That meant a lot of work over the weekend, but it was within the bounds of possibility for everyone except Nick—and Cady, given the additional work of the first witch.

There were groans but no complaints, and George pointed out, "What else is there to do when you're snowed in? There's more of it predicted for the weekend. So just stay home by your fires and learn lines, okay? We only have two more weeks till production week."

"Crazy to attempt Macbeth with so little rehearsal time," Cady observed to Nick as they put on boots and coats. "You'll hardly have all your lines down before opening night, Nick. You must be going mad."

"Well," he said, "it's not so bad. I played Macbeth not so long ago, in Edmonton. So it's just a case of brushing up."

"You did!" She felt a distinct sense of relief: there weren't many experiences more draining than being onstage with an actor who wasn't quite sure of his lines. "Oh, that's terrific! Actually, it's not so bad for me, either—I played Lady Macduff in England a few years ago, and it was one of those productions where we were all onstage the entire time, so deep in there—" she touched her temple "—is probably not just Lady Macbeth, but the entire play top to bottom."

"Everybody on stage throughout *Macbeth*?" Nick asked in the faint disbelief of someone who has seen everything and yet still vaguely hopes that some things are just not possible.

Cady laughed. "It wasn't so bad, really. We were all images called up by the witches—as if the whole play was a prediction or a vision they were seeing in their cave. It was quite interesting, really, the critics liked it. But boy, was it exhausting!"

"Who was your director?" he asked, and she told him, just as Jenny broke away from a chatting group and crossed to her side.

"Coming home, Cady?" she asked, and Cady looked at Nick and saw the danger of getting too close to him. Nick was a fast mover, of that she was quite certain, and in her current state she knew she should steer clear of any man who saw a sexual encounter as an ego-boosting conquest. She had had enough of that kind of man to last quite a while. She had had one too many.

"Sure thing," she said, grinning at Jenny. "Just let me get my boots on. See you Monday, Nick."

In spite of the snow, it seemed, there would always be cars on the road, but Cady knew she was what the locals called with contempt an "eastern driver" and she didn't think she could drive to Sturgis in such conditions. Instead, she spent most of her spare time and weekends on the city's buses, traveling from one neighborhood to another, getting off to walk whenever a street name plucked at a chord or the houses seemed somehow familiar.

She had a better memory for it all than she would have believed. The sight of a corner store would set her walking in a certain direction, turning corners with an almost unerring instinct, and there she would be, in front of a house where she had somehow got through two or three unhappy months before a harassed but determinedly cheerful social worker came to take her away.

Sometimes she found that whole blocks of an old neighborhood had disappeared. A huge business development stood on the site of one of her deepest humiliations: here, in the shadow of the huge glass-and-stone structure, she had stood under a maple tree long since chopped down, surrounded by a little girl named Missy—the "real" child of the house where she was fostered out—and all Missy's friends from the street. "Orphan" they had called her, and "bastard" and "nobody even wants to adopt her."

What odd forms revenge takes, Cady thought now, leaning back in the crisp cold prairie air to look up at the office building that had been the destruction of Missy's home and neighborhood and all that had been held just out of her reach in those days when she had yearned for security and love. *You see?* she told the eight-year-old self that inside her still stood under that tree, and still faced her tormentors with a face of stone. *You see?* She soothed the tears that had been inner tears only. *Noth-*

ing is permanent, not even other people's happiness. But the child was not comforted.

It was a painful, difficult time, and sometimes she did not understand what drove her to make this bitter pilgrimage into her past, which was becoming almost a compulsion with her.

It left those years of pain too near the surface, pain that clamored for expression. There came a day in rehearsal—a day when they were working through Act I, a heavy act for her—when she seemed to be sitting on a great caldron of turbulent emotion she couldn't control. No matter which of Lady Macbeth's emotions she reached into herself to find, what she came up with was pain. So all her readings were colored with a generalized emotion that meant nothing.

"Cady," George said to her after she had gone through the letter scene a couple of times, "you're like a scattergun. I want you to be a shotgun. One bullet, not a hundred useless pellets. You understand? Focus, Cady, focus. You got a lot of power in there, but you've got to aim it better before it'll have any effect on us. This is one focused lady we got here—she carries the whole enterprise and her husband along on the strength of her will, okay?"

The problem was that once she came onstage, Lady Macbeth scarcely left it till the end of the act. Cady got no breather the whole day, and no respite from Nick who, she realized suddenly, reminded her of Luke.

Late in the afternoon of that exhausting day it all came to a head. " 'What beast was't then,' " she demanded of Macbeth, " 'that made you break this enterprise to me?' " And suddenly she was remembering Luke and all the other deep disappointments of her life, all the times she had been offered something only to have it snatched away. She gave the whole speech in a tone of desperate, almost childlike disappointment, and ended it in tears.

so that Nick was forced to draw her into his arms to comfort her as she sobbed. Then he looked down at her and capitulated completely.

" 'If we should fail?' " asked Macbeth; but the battle was hers, she knew she had won.

" 'We fail?' " she demanded disbelievingly, wiping her tears and sniffing and rewarding him with a smile that was like the sun after a storm. " 'But screw your courage to the sticking-place and we'll not fail.' " Suddenly she was filled with excitement, plans and the certainty of success. " 'When Duncan is asleep....' "

"...and blackout," said Tom a few minutes later from his position beside George's chair. "And that's Act I. Thank you very much."

Nick breathed out to relieve his working tension and grinned down at Cady, where they stood just off the playing area that was marked with white tape on the floor. "Wooo, lady!" he said. "Are you really gonna do that to me every night?"

Cady laughed and wiped her eyes. "I don't know," she told him. "I didn't exactly have that planned."

George approached them. "Interesting," he said to Cady. "Interesting. A lot of power. I don't know if anyone's ever done a reading of Lady Macbeth like that. Okay." He didn't seem to know what to say. "Okay, that's it for today."

"The calls for tomorrow are up on the board," Tom informed the room in general. Most of the cast had already left, since the last scene had called for Cady and Nick only, but Banquo and Duncan, who had been in the previous scene, and one or two others had stayed to watch. "We start at the top of Act II at ten o'clock."

Cady went to check the board. Scene I was scheduled for an hour, so she herself wasn't called till eleven o'clock.

"You're quite a powerhouse," said Banquo, stopping

beside her, muffled up, on his way out. "George is right about focus, but wrong about the shotgun. You're more of a flamethrower."

Cady smiled at him, not sure if that was a compliment or not. "Well, I promise not to burn you."

"Oh, anytime," said Banquo. "Anytime."

Cady felt too restless to go home. She wrapped her scarf over her mouth and chin and set off instead in the direction of the city center, where an hour of browsing before closing time would calm the creative adrenaline running through her blood.

She found a mall that was warm and brightly lighted, and wandered aimlessly through. There were some dresses in a women's shop that she would have tried on if it weren't for the work of unwrapping all her winter gear; there was a smokeshop with odd little trinkets and mementos of Regina—good grief, did tourists really come to Regina in the winter? And there was a large, well set-up bookshop.

Cady turned in through the entrance. Bookshops were great places to browse. She had learned about books early in her childhood, and she had never lost her love of reading. There wasn't much you couldn't get from books. She wandered aimlessly, letting her eyes catch pictures and titles and section headings, stopping wherever her interest was caught.

She wandered past Occult, and Poetry, and Religion and Royalty—ever since the advent of Princess Diana, she noted with a smile, royalty had merited its own section again—and Science Fiction. Cady kept moving. There weren't many titles in Science Fiction because she was in the hardcover section, and most science fiction came out only in paperback. Luke had been right about the general contempt for the genre, she thought—it wasn't considered literature except for the classics. She saw Isaac Asimov's name, and a couple of Robert Heinlein's titles that she had read and disliked as a teenager, and Doris Lessing's Shikasta series. Cady paused. She had read that, and would have considered it literature well above the genre, but here it was in Science Fiction, with Larry Niven and Clifford Simak...and Luke Southam.

The Little Report, read the title, smaller than and underneath his name, glaring white on a black background. He must be a "name" all right, Cady thought absently. The unexpected sight of his name affected her not at all. He had hurt her, that was all she associated with his name, but she was used to being hurt. She no longer remembered the closeness he had made her feel, nor the love she had thought she felt for him, nor any yearning to be loved. It was mild curiosity only that motivated her to pick up the book.

"A classic of postapocalypse scenarios!"—*N.Y. Times*, read some smaller print.

Cady opened the book slowly, flipping past the title page to a page which read, "The sky is falling."—Chicken Little.

She laughed. *The "Little" Report*, indeed! Well, he had a sense of humor, she knew that. He'd never stopped making her laugh. Cady closed the book with a little snap and dropped it back on the shelf, then turned and eyed the walls of the shop, where the shelves of paperbacks were.

No longer browsing, Cady moved decisively over to the science-fiction paperback section. Here the authors and titles were a hundred times more numerous, and Luke Southam's name appeared above five or six titles. Cady picked up one copy of each title automatically, then paused guiltily. She really shouldn't be reading anything but Macbeth at the moment. She put back everything except *The Little Report* and *The Man Who Saved Time in a Bottle*; then smiled, shook her head and dutifully put even them back, turning from the shelf at last empty-handed. She had a lot of work to do before opening night. There would be plenty of time for reading after November 26. She would have three weeks of free days during the run.

It was a good argument, and valid. Its momentum carried her almost to the mall entrance before she stopped and turned back again to the shelves holding Luke's books.

8

"Do you do this a lot?" Luke asked curiously.

Dee's eyes swept the room ceaselessly, discontentedly, taking in the people at other tables, the newcomers, checking, checking. He was discontented because his hungry gaze found nothing to feed upon, but he could not kick the watching habit. "Hey!" he demanded aggrievedly, turning full face to Luke for the first time that night. "I'm only here 'cause you twisted my arm! Man, you dragged me here!"

"I know, I know," said Luke placatingly. "But I just wondered. It's so—" He glanced around the warmly lighted room, where several dozen actors and performers ate, drank, table-hopped, smiled vicious smiles and sometimes took to the onstage piano to favor the company with a little talent. The room was a well-known dinner theater that after hours opened its doors to members of the theatrical community, a place for seeing and being seen. Luke could enjoy the ad hoc entertainment, and he was, as a writer, generally a people-watcher. But there was an air of grim gaiety in the room, and the sound of human hypocrisy fell constantly on his ears; and he was as a result restless, bored and critical. "It reminds me too much of L.A.," he finished apologetically.

"L.A.!" Dee repeated incredulously. "Man, this is nothing like L.A.! Not a pale shadow. Hell, in L.A. there are always people, you know? I mean, there are *people* to *see*."

Luke grinned and relapsed into silence, letting his eyes rove the room again, searching the faces, feeling almost as experienced as Dee in his awareness of movement and new arrivals.

He was looking for Cady. He had been to more parties in the past month than in his entire life previously, he sometimes thought. Always theatrical parties, always forcing poor old Dee to drag him along.

At first he had casually asked people if they knew an actress named Cady, but they had looked at him so suspiciously that he stopped doing so. Sometimes he would say casually to someone he had met before, "Seen Cady lately?" But they invariably asked him, Katy who? If he spelled the name out it got embarrassing, because invariably they hadn't heard of her, so how did he think they knew her? He had learned to say simply, "Oh, sorry, I was thinking of someone else."

It was less difficult not to ask but simply to watch, searching the faces, hoping that the countless faces he examined for traces of her would not dull the bright image of her face he carried in his mind. It would be ironic if one day he bumped into her and no longer recognized her.

Dee never table-hopped. He never had to. There was apparently a rigid code in such things—a lesser mortal came to the table of a greater, but never vice versa. That would be losing face. Dee was one of the most powerful men in the room, by his own reckoning. He was well-known and successful, on his way up. He had connections in all the right places. In Los Angeles there were tables he would have visited, but here the world came to him.

Or half the world, at least. The half that knew he was working on a project and who put getting work above all other considerations. The other half resented the intrusion of an outsider into their ranks—especially a

successful American whom they saw as throwing his
weight around—and this half ignored his table.

Cady, Luke apostrophized inside his head, *if you
are out of work, and I know you must be, why the hell
aren't you here cultivating my friend Dee?*

Dee was his drawing card. With Dee he could be sure
of seeing the entire theatrical community of Toronto
sooner or later.

So he had told himself, in the early days; but now it
seemed more like later than sooner, and where was
Cady? Where the hell was Cady?

"Hi, there!" said a raspy, humorous female voice, and
he looked up to see a couple he had bumped into at several parties and talked to without being introduced, and
who were now obviously using the acquaintance to
glean an introduction to Dee. Luke obliged. It didn't
bother him; he knew it was the way people in this
business survived—and anyway, wasn't he using everyone he could to glean an introduction to Cady?

"You must have caught Bernard's show at the Royal
Alex," he told Dee by way of introduction. If he were as
helpful as he could be, perhaps God would reward him
with a little help? Lord, he'd further anybody's career if
it meant.... "And Thea's in a revue called, I think,
Standing Room Only?" He looked to her for confirmation, and she grinned at him.

"Yeah! You've seen it, right?"

"Right," said Luke. "I enjoyed it very much, too.
You're a very funny lady. I noticed you particularly—
and another actor, a man who started out the evening
young and ended up so old and decrepit I—"

He stopped because she was laughing, as though at
some private joke. "You enjoyed that, did you?" she
nodded. "Yeah, the audience loved that bit. He doesn't
do it anymore," she added with satisfaction. "Not anymore at all."

She was very adept at including Dee in the conversation, he noted, so that after a few minutes, when she said to him, "You're in town to do a film?" It seemed like polite interest, not in the least pushy.

But Dee nodded and looked as though he expected the inevitable pitch.

She said, "I thought it fell through—didn't it fall through? Or is this a new project you're working on?"

Dee looked pained, and it occurred to Luke suddenly that except for that similar sense of humor and their dedication to their work, he and Dee had little in common. He didn't always like Dee. Yet they had been fast friends from their first meeting. That was kind of interesting, he thought—something to explore someday.

"No, it's not a new project," Dee told the woman, looking irritably up at her through the smoke of his cigarette. "It's the same film I've always planned on doing."

Her looked became fixed. "It is?" she demanded, bending a little closer. "Say, that's great! I heard you ran into problems—"

"We've had a small delay," Dee said with an air of putting down pretension. "In the film world, there are always delays."

But the sandy-haired actress was irrepressible. "So are you finished casting? When do you start the shoot?"

"I haven't finalized the casting," he admitted with magnaminity. "We go out to the location after Christmas."

At that point the couple were edged aside by a stunning blonde. "*Darling!*" she cried in a trilling voice. "Where have you been? You told me you'd be in town right through November, but you *weren't* . . . !"

Bernard's lips twitched as he threw a farewell wave to Luke and took his lady's arm to lead her away. Luke lifted his hand to them, but Thea had forgotten his existence.

"Did you hear that?" she was saying excitedly to her sweetheart. "I've got to call...."

Her voice faded into the general hubbub and with a guilty start Luke returned his gaze to the room, searching, searching....

THEIR FIRST REHEARSAL ONSTAGE was the most problem-ridden technical Cady had ever sat through, and she had the additional difficulty of costume to contend with. Normally she wouldn't wear dress for a technical, but Lady Macbeth's costumes were barbaric and heavy, and she wanted to get used to them—and to her rapid costume changes. So she sat by the lighted director's table in the center of the house, her feet ungainly sprawled on the balcony railing in front of her, the heavy costume pulled up over her knees, waiting for her next scene. She was immersed in a book. Not a final study of her lines, either, like the good actress she was, but a copy of Luke Southam's *The Man Who Saved Time in a Bottle—And Other Stories*.

As she came to the end of a story Cady set down the book and stretched, then took a look at the action.

"Can you bring up preset number two here, please?" George Talousien was saying into the small mike that had been mounted on his temporary desk in the front row of the balcony. He was hooked up by intercom to the lighting man's booth and the stage manager, and there weren't many directors, Cady had come to realize, who had George's technical knowledge and his determination to get exactly the effect he wanted.

"Okay, can you take it up another two points, please? Okay, it looks too cold now. Can you dim down preset seven? Yeah, yeah, a bit more. What? Yeah. Okay, then, eighty-six the blue altogether. That's right, all of it. Yeah. I want a nice home atmosphere here. Right. All right. That's it, will you mark that?" He made a note, then turned to the stage again. "All right, Tom."

"Okay, Jenny." Tom poked his head out from the wings. "Can we cut to where you cue the murderers now, please?"

Jenny looked up from where she had been lounging patiently in the living room of her ancient Celtic castle. " 'Poor prattler,' is that what you want?"

"Murderers, is that your cue?" called Tom.

A shadowy face appeared from the wings on stage right. "We've been taking Annette's last line as our cue, Tom."

"Okay, from Annette's speech then." He consulted his S.M.'s script. "From the top of that speech, Annette, okay? So from, 'If he were dead.' "

Annette made a little skipping motion onstage. A small slight actress, she was playing both the second witch and Fleance as well as Lady Macduff's young son, and had some pretty wild costume changes of her own.

"I'm never gonna make it," she had direly informed Cady and Jenny in the dressing room. "George is crazy if he thinks I can. I swear those guys are gonna come on and murder Lady Macduff and a witch!"

But like most theatrical difficulties it would be worked out somehow—probably by the actress's own ingenuity. Although George envisioned all the witches in near nudity, Annette had privately warned the designer that she was likely to need a full flowing robe of some sort for the scene immediately prior to the murder scene because she was going to have to wear the young boy's costume underneath. But George wouldn't be presented with that problem till tomorrow afternoon's technical dress.

Annette hopped around the stage now on one leg, holding the other up behind by the ankle. " 'If he were dead,'" she told Lady Macduff saucily, "'you'd weep for him. If not, it were a good sign that I should quickly have a new father.'"

"Okay, is that your cue, murderers?" Tom called. He looked at George. "Are you taking that lighting change from here?"

Cady reached for her book and stood up, making her way along the row to the aisle. At this rate it would take another year to get to the sleep-walking scene. Yawning in boredom, she walked through the theater and back to the green room.

"How's it going?" an actor sitting with a group playing cards asked her. The PA system was on, he could hear for himself, but still someone coming from the actual scene, like a war reporter, was expected to have a certain insight.

Cady flung herself into a chair. "It's not," she informed him succinctly. "If we get through this technical tonight it'll be a miracle." She leaned back, picked up her book and flipped it open at the next story.

"The Raccoon Conspiracy," she read, and there was a tiny, unmistakable tug at her heart. She had read half the book, and she was wishing she could throw it away, because every story was Luke. Every word brought him back to her mind, the gentleness, the passion, the humor—and the happiness he had made her feel. His words on paper were busily tearing down all the defenses she had built up against the memory of those few golden days, and the love that had been born in her. Cady knew she was letting herself in for more hurt, that she should stop reading the book, but as with trusting and loving Luke the first time, the temptation was too sweet. In spite of all the subsequent pain, the memory of love still warmed her heart; and her heart had been cold a long, long time.

"The Raccoon Conspiracy" was a silly, amusing

story, a sort of brief world history from the raccoons' point of view, describing their long patient wait to take control of Earth after centuries of painstaking sabotage. But their worldview was warped. The "coffers of wealth" the raccoons constantly pillaged the reader was suddenly made aware, were nothing more than picnic coolers. Everything the raccoons saw as a major victory was in fact something small and silly from mankind's point of view. You couldn't help being charmed by their misguided zeal and determination, and Cady set the book down for a moment, chuckling softly.

They were running the last scene of Act IV entirely— there must be a lot of internal cues—and the actors' voices booming through the PA system were making it difficult to concentrate. She remembered instead the morning when she and Luke had awakened to a campsite that had been pillaged by raccoons, and the ridiculous way Luke had carried on.

The tug at her heart became stronger and began to hurt in earnest. Cady closed her eyes, trying to ride the pain, trying to calm her breathing against the unexpected sharpness of the daggers in her heart.

Oh Luke, she thought hopelessly. *I loved you, Luke, I really did. I've been lying to myself, pretending that I knew all along it was going to end. But I didn't know. I was hoping, I was always hoping, Luke....*

"What," boomed a deep resonant voice from the loudspeaker, "*all my little chickens and their dam in one fell swoop?*" and she remembered more sharply than ever, remembered Luke desperately clinging to his cornflakes box and the two dirty bits of white bread, shouting his ridiculous paraphrase of that line, making her laugh, making her heart contract with the pain of too much joy.

She began to laugh, and the laughter turned to tears so suddenly that the wild sob burst from her before she

knew that she had stopped laughing. She jumped up, a
hand over her mouth, and ran from the room, fighting
down the sobs.

"Cady?" said a startled male voice from the green
room as the door closed behind her. "Cady, are you all
right?" But the gentle concern in the tone only made it
worse.

WHILE THUNDER BOOMED AND CRACKED and the lighting
did several strange things at once, Cady whirled in a
slow circle, unbuttoning her heavy Lady Macbeth costume, which Nick had dubbed "standard issue Celtic
primitive" but which was nevertheless very beautiful.
As she let it slide to the ground the huge smoking
caldron rose up through the floor of the stage in front of
her. Still whirling, now to the accompaniment of other
odd and various sounds of nature, she slowly undid her
thick black braids, trying to get them to unravel into a
free-flowing head of hair. It wasn't going to work. For a
start the caldron was stuck half in and half out of the
floor, and wouldn't budge.

" 'Thrice the brinded cat hath mewed,' " she chanted,
and then collapsed into giggles. She turned toward the
house where a tiny light behind the glow of the lamps
showed her where the director sat.

"George," she said, standing like *Venus Disrobed* in
the mound of fur and leather at her feet, a black rag
delicately draping her body and her hair half braided
and half free. "George." She heard a few giggles and
stifled snorts from different parts of the house and
wings, and a cursing stagehand under the caldron,
and she tried manfully to stifle her own amusement.
"George," she tried again, "don't you think this is a bit
too much like Wonder Woman?"

That did it. Everybody—cast, crew, costume people,
S.M.—burst into uncontrollable laughter, relieving

all the tension that had been building through the day.

It was a disastrous technical dress. Everybody said it would be impossible to pull the show together by tomorrow night's opening. It was nearly beyond the realm of possibility that they would be ready for a dress-rehearsal tonight. And there were bound to be outsiders at the dress, Jenny had told her; George always invited a few people along.

When the laughter died, George called from the bowels of the theater with great dignity, "What exactly is the problem, Cady?"

"There's more than one problem, actually, George," she told him. "First, this robe is so heavy that I can't throw it away from me when it comes off, so here it is all wrapped around my feet." Snorts and muffled laughter from all around the theater. Everybody was punch-drunk with strain and fatigue, Cady realized, including herself. They had been going nonstop since 9:00 A.M., and heaven knew how long before that George and Tom had begun.

"Also this black cobweb I'm wearing catches on everything, George, so I'm a little concerned about ending up stark naked here. And then my wig. George, you just can't unravel this much hair in a few—"

"All right, all right." George was coming down through the stalls toward the stage. He wasn't at the little lighted station she had been blindly directing all her comments toward. "Costume! Is there someone from costume around?"

A blue-jeaned redhead stepped out from the wings, incongruous against the primitive set, which was frozen halfway between Scottish castle and witches' cavern.

"Cathy," said George, "why won't this wig unplait?"

She shrugged. "Well, it would, George, if she had enough time. It's just that a minute isn't enough time to do the change."

"All right, Cady, can you start to do that with your hair earlier? During the previous scene, once all the company leaves?"

Cady looked at him. "My husband has just seen the ghost of the man he's murdered and made the whole kingdom suspicious and all I can think of to do is comb my hair?" she asked unbelievingly.

"Okay, Cathy, why is her costume so heavy?"

Cathy gave vent to a helpless snort of laughter. "Because you wanted it to look authentic, George. Do you know how much work went into the thing?"

"George," Cady called. "Could I suggest something?" He looked at her. "Why don't I go off left with Nick at the end of the banquet scene—then there'd be someone to help with the costume change and my hair? And I could come back on from center back. That way there'll be no danger of me tripping over my costume or the caldron and falling in on top of all the Apparitions."

George pursed his lips. He did not like the idea, but something had to give or they were looking at certain disaster, opening night and every night of the run. And a comic disaster was not what the play needed at the top of Act IV, when tragedy was beginning to close in.

"All right," said George, "it's not going to work, is that it? You can't humanly make that change?" Cady shook her head. "Okay, Tom!" George called. The stage manager appeared from his station stage left. "Tom, if we shift the interval to the end of Act III, how does that affect the crew and set changes?"

"It would make it a lot easier, actually," said Tom delicately, clearly afraid that if he showed too much relief it would put George off. "It's easier to set up the banquet scene on the run and strike it at our leisure during the interval." The stagehands had been muttering about this awkward set change for days. "Actually, that would kill the problem with the caldron here, too. We

could have it there from the top of the second half, just
like the first. Those Apparitions could be all ready to
go. . . ."

So it was solved, to Cady's and the crew's utter relief.
After such a major compromise, George seemed to
make the smaller ones more readily, and they got
through the technical only two hours late, one hour
before the dress rehearsal was scheduled to go up.

Cady sank into her chair in front of her makeup mirror, giggling and relieved, and feeling the beginnings of
opening-night tension start in her stomach.

"Thank you all for a good technical dress," Tom's
calm voice came over the PA system. "Tonight's dress is
being delayed until eight o'clock. Will you all please
relax, go out for a meal and be back here for seven-
thirty? The half-hour call is at seven-thirty. Thank
you. . . ."

"THIS IS YOUR FIVE-MINUTE CALL, ladies and gentlemen,
five minutes. Places, please. Your five-minute call.
Places, please. Let's have a good show."

Tonight the voice was low, almost a whisper, and
behind it through the PA system came the noise of
voices and laughter, the noise of an opening-night audience. The tension that had begun in Cady yesterday
was in full flower now as she stood in front of the dressing room's full-length mirror and cast a last glance over
the black cobwebby costume, her body makeup, the
long black hair flowing over her shoulders and back,
down past her waist. *Let it not catch on anything*, she
prayed, *I don't want my wig coming off in the middle of
a scene.*

"It's a full house," said Jenny, appearing beside her in
similar costume, and Cady's stomach clenched and
knotted. "Ready to go up?"

"Where's Annette?" Cady asked, both of them whispering, though in the dressing rooms whispering was unnecessary.

"She's up there. Let's go."

And then they were standing in the wings, watching the house lights go dim as the audience quieted and settled down into expectancy. Blackout. Together the three witches crept onstage and took up their positions while thunder cracked and lightning flashed. A faint light bathed the three women and the thunder died, and the nervous tension left Cady in a rush. Look at them, hundreds of them, waiting for her to speak, waiting to be moved by *her*. Hundreds, and she *would* move them. They might love her or hate her, but they would not be indifferent to her.

When the light was at its level the first witch looked up through the screen of her hair and laughed at the thunder. " 'When shall we three meet again?' " she wondered. " 'In thunder, lightning, or in rain?' "

THE OPENING-NIGHT PARTY lasted till the small hours, the entire cast and crew loud and excitable with the burn-off of the past days of pressure and tension, and consumed with curiosity about the reviews. The national paper, the *Globe and Mail*, hadn't been in the audience, but the local paper had been, and a weekly. Fortunately or unfortunately the next day was Sunday, so no review would appear till Monday's paper.

So there was no point staying up all night to wait for the reviews, Cady was told, you just stayed up to stay up.

Still, it all had to come to an end sometime, and when it did Jenny went off with Nick, with whom she had started a raging affair a week or two ago, Tom went Cady knew not where—and Cady went home alone. She let herself silently into the house and crept up the stairs so as not to wake Mrs. Manning, and into her lonely room.

But Mrs. Manning wasn't asleep. She was sitting quietly in the chair in Cady's room, with a small lamp glowing on the table beside her.

"Oh!" Cady whispered. "Sorry, I forgot." She turned to go, but Mrs. Manning's quiet voice called her back.

"No, it's all right, dear," she said. "It's so late now. Come in."

Cady crossed the room to the dressing table and sat, absentmindedly picking up a brush and running it through her hair. Most of her cosmetic and night things were in the small back bedroom. She waited.

"Well, he didn't come," said Mrs. Manning matter-of-factly, stretching a little as though she had sat in the same position for too long. Which she must have done, Cady realized. She had probably been there since ten o'clock last night.

"I'm sorry," she commiserated softly, and she was. Perhaps it was the lateness of the hour, but somehow tonight the house felt lonely; and the idea of Mrs. Manning sitting up to watch for the ghost of her dead husband no longer seemed so farfetched as it had earlier. Now it seemed only poignant.

"I think Mrs. Manning's going to ask if she can sit in your room Saturday night," Jenny had confided one day early in the week. "November 26 is Rusty Manning's night."

That was how Cady had discovered that she was sleeping in a room that had its very own ghost. Rusty Manning had died nearly twenty years ago, but it was only in the years since Mrs. Manning had started renting out rooms that his ghost had been seen—at odd times, by different people, but always here, in the old master bedroom.

Mrs. Manning herself had never seen him, but she still

hoped. And November 26 was a significant date to her and Rusty, the date when she obviously felt she would be most likely to see him, though she had never told anyone why. On that night, in latter years, she had begun to watch. If the room was unrented, or if the occupant was someone who seemed, like Cady, level-headed, Mrs. Manning sat up all night for him. Cady had agreed to spend tonight—and every subsequent night if Rusty appeared, she had privately promised herself—in the bedroom at the back of the house, so that Mrs. Manning could watch. But at the last moment, forgetting, she had barged in.

If Mrs. Manning was disappointed at being disturbed, she didn't show it. She stood up now, an ordinary, matter-of-fact, gray-haired woman, and said in her ordinary voice, "I'd like a cup of coffee. How about you?"

There was a kind of plea in that, and Cady agreed instantly. "Decaffeinated." And as if by instinct the two lonely women headed for the most comforting room in the house and that most comforting of all sounds—a whistling kettle, and sat down to talk about Mrs. Manning's loving husband.

"He always appears naked, they tell me," Mrs. Manning told Cady with a grin as they sat enjoying the warmth and comfort of the kitchen. "And only ever to women. He always had a sense of humor, Rusty did."

Cady eyed her in laughing alarm. "I don't suppose he's ever actually got into bed with anyone?" she asked faintly.

"Well, you know, he's never done that," and there was a faint regret in Mrs. Manning's tone. "No, mostly he just stands there, and whenever anyone goes back to investigate, he's gone." She stood up, took the whistling kettle off the range and made tea. "We enjoyed the bed-room, Rusty and I—that's what first made me think it

must be him. Oh, we really enjoyed the bedroom." She
smiled at Cady. "They talk a lot of rubbish these days,
but one thing I'm glad of for today's young people—sex
is so much freer, isn't it? It's considered natural nowadays. It wasn't like that when Rusty and I were young,
but well...we were lucky enough to be suited that way.
And I'll always say, Cady, that a good love life is half
the battle in a marriage. If you've got sex...well, if you
don't have sex, your differences can just eat you up—
drive you apart. I've seen that happen. But no matter
how hard we fought, Rusty and I could always find our
way back to each other."

She smiled reminiscently, looking at Cady. "You
know, over the years I've noticed something I've never
told anyone. Rusty only ever appears to the girls he
would have thought sexy—dark girls with good
bodies—like I was. Like you. I like to think that's our
little private joke—his and mine." She looked at Cady
speculatively. "When I first saw you I thought perhaps—" She broke off.

"Well, don't you go marrying a man unless he thrills
you, Cady, a man who just makes you open right up to
him, body and heart. A man who'll give you memories
enough to keep you warm after he's gone, if necessary."
She paused. "Someday memories may be all you have.
But if you find the right man, memories are all you
need. You know, I can't understand it—with all the ex-
perimenting you young people are allowed to do these
days, I see just as many mismatched couples as there
ever were. Don't you be mismatched, Cady. You find
yourself a man you can *really* love."

By the time she sank into bed—in the cot in the tiny
room beside the bathroom—Cady was close to tears.
Everybody had someone: Jenny had Nick, even if only
temporarily, Tom had his unknown friend, even Mrs.
Manning had memories and a husband who still watched

over her.... "A man who'll give you memories," she had said, "a man who makes you open up body and heart...."

But Cady had always avoided memories, because to her the past was a place of pain. She had learned early to forget: to forget the bad times because the memory hurt; to forget the good times because that hurt, too—remembering what you had lost.

When she had lost Luke, habit had taken over, pushing him out of her mind, pushing him down into the areas below consciousness, to where he could not hurt her.

Luke, oh Luke. Her heart was suddenly aching with the hurt she had never let herself feel. Luke. She had found him, with his sometimes gentle, sometimes passionate understanding and need of her—she had found him, and what had he said? "I live with a woman, Cady...."

Suddenly the memory of his touch was harsh on her body, making her gasp with need, making her lonelier and needier than she had ever been in her life.

"Luke," she whispered aloud, her voice filled with despair. For her magic defenses no longer worked—not against Luke. She couldn't pretend anymore, she couldn't shut out the knowledge.

She loved him. She needed him. She had found her one true lover. And right now he was probably planning a Christmas wedding with another woman.

IT WAS ONLY A FEW HOURS LATER that the household was jarred awake by the shrilling of the telephone. Cady looked at her watch, grunted and rolled over. Nine o'clock on a Sunday morning? *Shoot the sod*, she thought, burying her head in the pillow.

"Cady," Mrs. Manning's voice called up the back stairs. "Caa-dee."

At nine o'clock on a Sunday morning? Cady rolled up on one elbow and was momentarily surprised by her surroundings. What was she doing in this little room? Oh yes, the ghost. She hadn't wanted to sleep with Mrs. Manning's dead husband, no matter how sexy he was.

Some residue of the night's strangeness buzzed along her spine. Who could be calling her at this hour?

"Cady, telephone."

She staggered out of bed cursing and, not bothering with a robe, trailed through the chilly house in her rumpled pajamas.

"Hello?" she demanded grumpily.

"Is that Cady Hunter?" asked a light female voice.

She thought it was the long-distance operator. "Yes, yes," she said urgently, "this is Cady Hunter."

"Cady, you probably don't remember me," said the voice, "but we used to be best friends a long, long time ago. My name is Shirley Woznicki, and we—"

"Shirley!" she cried. "Shirley!"

The voice chuckled. "You remember me."

"Of course I remember! Shirley, my gosh, Shirley from Sturgis, right?" She hardly waited for confirmation. "I couldn't remember your last name, but I meant to go to Sturgis and look you up. We just opened last night, I was going to come—"

"I know you did." Shirley laughed. "I just heard it on Arts Calendar. Congratulations! It's a good thing I heard it, because I don't live in Sturgis anymore."

"Where are you?"

"Right here in Regina. I'd love to see you again. I'd like to see your show, too."

Cady was laughing and crying. "Come tonight," she said. "It'll be a terrible show, it's second night tonight, but come anyway, okay?"

"Okay."

"Come backstage afterward and we'll talk—we can go out for a drink and talk. Is that okay?"

"It's okay. But listen, Cady—where the hell did you go? One day you just weren't there at school—my parents told me you'd gone away. Where did you go?"

"My grandparents were killed," Cady told her. "Didn't they tell you that? The social workers came and picked me up and brought me to Regina. It was always the social workers."

"Isn't that a funny coincidence? I'm a social worker now, Cady," Shirley's voice came down the wire. "I work with problem kids. I always wondered why I was drawn to it—maybe it was because of you. Isn't it strange?"

"Yes, it's strange," said Cady, quietly absorbing it. "It really is. All my life I've hated social workers. All my life. And all my life I've remembered you and thought of you as my friend. And now here you are, and you're a social worker."

She wanted to make Shirley understand, but language seemed to be inadequate to the job, and Cady stopped speaking helplessly. "You'll think I'm mad," she said, "but it's nine o'clock and I've had a rough night." She laughed self-deprecatingly.

"No, I don't think you're mad," said Shirley. "I understand—I'm a social worker, and you hate social workers but you don't hate me. Yeah, that's something to deal with, Cady, but it'll be good for you, won't it?"

"I guess so," said Cady.

"Sure it will," laughed Shirley. "Go back to sleep now, sorry to wake you. I'll see you tonight."

But it didn't seem as though sleep was on the cards for Cady that morning. She was only halfway up the stairs when the phone rang again.

"Miss Cady Hunter, please." This time it was the operator. "Long distance calling."

"Cady?" demanded Thea's gravelly voice down the wire when she had identified herself. "Hiya, kid, how's things?"

"We opened last night," said Cady.

"Did you! Congratulations! How'd it go?"

"They loved it," Cady told her with a reminiscent grin. "The audiences out here really love George—the crazier he gets, the better they like it." And they'd been wide awake, too, which had surprised Cady. When she had come out as Lady Macbeth, after her first appearance as the witch, there had been gasps of recognition through the house.

"Good for them!" applauded Thea. "I like an audience with an adventurous spirit! So—now you're all happily hung over and—what time is it out there?"

"Quarter past nine."

"Ouch! Well, never mind, I've been sitting on this since midnight last night, and it's noon here! Listen, kid, Miles Davidson is back in town! And he's got *Love and Regret* going again, same as before. *Just* the same as before, you got that?"

"Got it," said Cady dumbly.

"Yeah, well, you get off your little ass and on the blower tomorrow and you call him, right? Because the casting isn't finalized yet, so you just might be still in the running. And don't, *don't* tell him you're in Regina, okay? I mean, he's bound to wonder, right? Put him off with some story, but don't tell him you're playing Lady Macbeth in the provinces, okay? Listen to me now."

"I'm listening."

"Good. This is costing a fortune. If I'd known you'd answer the phone yourself I would have dialed direct."

"Did he call me?"

"What? No, no, that's what makes it so important! You gotta call, remind him. Directors forget too damn easy. No, hey—I got the news straight from the horse's you-know-what!''

"I didn't know you knew Miles."

"Honey." Thea's voice was dry. "I know everybody when I have to. Gotta go! Bernie's waiting. Bye now!"

Cady set the receiver back on the hook through the banisters and sat there on the step, thinking. Miles back in town, working on the same project. What a piece of luck that was! But Thea was right—directors' memories were short. And she had three more weeks to stick it out here.

Thea was right, she shouldn't have come. She would have to think of something that would make Miles content to wait for her. She'd have to dream up a dying mother or something. . . .

There was one good side to all this—after all this time there was just the possibility that Miles Davidson would have forgotten the weekend up on the French River. Maybe by this time he would have a lady he wouldn't want to cheat on. Maybe now he would be strictly business.

Maybe pigs would fly.

9

LUKE PULLED A CAN OF COKE from the fridge, walked into his living room, picked up the remote-control television switch, flung himself down onto his white sofa and pressed the On button, with all the air of a man starting an unbearably tedious job in a factory.

He hated television. It was the only junk food that he did hate, but he hated it thoroughly. He hated it up, down and sideways.

He hated drama shows, private-eye shows and soap operas. He hated game shows and cop shows and he hated commercials. He hated mystery shows and tv movies. But most particularly he hated comedy shows and their unremitting canned laughter.

He hadn't known before how *much* he hated it all, because before he had rarely watched television. He had sometimes watched news, and now and then an important tennis match or the Canada-Russia hockey series; or he had caught a feature film or an interesting documentary. And once or twice he had watched some British import when he needed to get his mind off his work, and that wasn't so bad.

Now all of his least horrible choices were closed to him. It was no use watching news, or documentaries, or hockey, or feature films, or even the current British series that he thought he might have been able to stomach. No, Luke thought darkly, he had to watch Canadian comedy and Canadian drama. Luke checked his guide for which channel was dealing with its Canadian content just then and flipped the channel changer lazily but with a subdued angry tension.

"When I finally do find you, Cady," he addressed the air loudly, "you are going to pay for every minute I have wasted in front of this damned mindless box. Do you hear? Every minute."

When he found the channel he flung down the remote control and reached for his Coke. There had been another call from his editor today, wondering where his new book was.

"Still in my head," he had informed her gently. "Where it is likely to stay forever unless you get off my back."

His sweet temper had deserted him weeks ago, he realized vaguely. He was as irritable and unpredictable as an addict coming off something pleasant but debilitating. *Oh, well,* he thought resignedly, *it could have been worse. I might have been forced to watch* American *situation comedy.*

He turned his attention finally to the set and absentmindedly stuck his finger in the Coke-tin loop to pull.

Then he stopped dead, jerking his eyes to the screen. He made a sound like choking, dropped the Coke can to the floor and jumped to a half-standing, half-sitting position, frozen into immobility.

"Cady!" he coughed hoarsely. "Cady, my God, finally!" His eyes riveted to the screen, he sank into his seat, looking and listening with all his attention. If a bomb had destroyed everything in that moment except himself and the television set, he would not have noticed.

She was there, beautiful, her hands in that magnificent hair piled up on her head, and somewhere a man was speaking in a tired, bored voice. "George was having problems in Montreal," he was saying; he was talking about business, the day he'd had. Only Cady was in view, beautiful Cady with a tiny lacy camisole just showing at the bottom of the screen, just covering that smooth velvet skin, the fullness of those breasts.

". . . going to have to send a team there," continued the man's voice, and Cady pulled a pin from her hair, and then another. "I'll have to look after it myself . . ." he went on. And then Cady pulled another pin from her hair, and the voice faltered, hesitated and stopped speaking altogether as though she finally impinged on his consciousness as the black cloud of her hair fell down, down her back, down around her shoulders and cheeks; the beautiful, black sweet-scented cloud that Luke had known. . . .

The man's voice changed. "Hey, you know something?" he said softly then. "I missed you," and Cady smiled a slow smile and turned her eyes toward her off-camera man, knowing she had the power to move him.

Luke was suddenly galvanized out of stupefaction. "Video!" he shouted. "My God, I have to record—" And he flung himself full length along the sofa, reaching for the remote control of the video recorder. He knocked over a small table that held a lamp and other odd breakables, and barked his knee painfully in the process. But Cady's face was already gone from the screen, replaced by a shot of the product. Shampoo, Luke saw. And a woman's voice whispered the secret of the brand-name to the millions of women watching.

Luke lay outstretched in the debris of his living room, half on the sofa, half on the floor, clutching the video control in his outstretched hand, listening to the machine click into action just as a Xerox commercial flashed on the screen. He crawled back through the litter of the upended table to his seat on the sofa and reached for the television remote control with one hand as he rubbed his wounded knee with the other. With a sense of thrilling power, as though he were executing a hated enemy, he lifted the control box to within range and pressed the Off button. Silence descended around his ears so perfectly that he laughed.

"Ah, Cady," he said quietly, reaching absentmindedly for the bright red can of Coke that rolled on the floor between his feet. "I have got you now." Lifting the can up, he found the loop of the opener with his forefinger and snapped if off. "I have got—"

Coca-Cola rocketed out of the can in a jet stream of bubbles, spraying Luke's chest and face and the wall and fountaining up in a fine, wide spray almost to the ceiling before it rained down again—on him, on the television set and the upended table; on the beautiful white carpet, and, most thickly, on his white sofa.

Luke sat in the soft acid rainfall amid the destruction of his living room without moving, and breathed a deep, deep breath.

"Cady," he promised softly, shaking his head, "when I get you, girl. When I get my hands on you. . . ."

As the days went by and all the merchants of the nation began to hype up their Christmas displays and advertising and their forced goodwill to all people, she became more and more convinced that this Christmas Luke would be marrying Sharon. Many weddings took place around Christmas, she had read once, because of the income-tax deduction to be gained that way.

And at Christmas everyone felt a kind of general love and goodwill, didn't they? Ever since she was a child Cady had felt that Christmas was a big, happy secret that she was forever left out of. Everyone was with family at Christmas, everyone felt loving and kind; salesclerks smiled and wished you Merry Christmas. . . .

If there was family pressure, and pressure from Sharon, and even pressure from Luke's own need to love—how could he get by without marrying Sharon?

Her dream, the dream she had had during that first

terrible time after leaving him, came back to haunt her
in waking live. It had seemed so real, to be standing
there and watching Luke marry someone else. Sometimes she believed that she was telepathically linked to
him, and that he had actually been getting married
while she'd had the dream. She had felt the pain so deeply.

She felt a sometimes overwhelming regret that she
hadn't stayed and tried to win Luke, and she was afraid
that it was a regret she would feel all her life. But try as
she might, she could not imagine anything permanent
with him; she knew that she was alone and somehow
would always be so. And in spite of what Mrs. Manning
had said, surely she would be happier if she didn't have
memories to torment her? What was the point of loving
if you were going to lose anyway?

Reading Luke's books—and she read them all—was
half torment, half joy. The torment was what she would
always feel, on the outside looking in; the joy, she
knew, was a gift from Luke. He had opened her heart
that much, that she had experienced sharing and love.
Whatever she did now, she was a little more complete as
a person; she had at least had the courage, once upon a
time, to love and let herself be loved.

And that gave her the courage to seek out her past, to
let it touch her. It gave her the strength to make the long
journey back toward herself that, under Luke's gui-
dance, she had begun—a journey that had, she knew
now, brought her here to Regina, where all her ghosts
lived.

Except one. Margery Simpson was a living ghost, and
where she was living now was anyone's guess. One day
Cady set out to track down the Simpsons. She visited
the neighboring houses on Randolf Street, in the vain
search for someone still living there from the time of the
Simpsons. She called the firm where George Simpson

had worked, in Regina and then in Vancouver, but George had long since left the company and there were no records to show where he had gone. She checked the telephone listings of Vancouver, but there were pages of Simpsons, even of G. Simpsons.

Perhaps Margery Simpson was one ghost that she could never lay to rest, but if so, there were plenty of others to work on. And Cady did work, digging deep into memory, both inside herself and in the city of her past, to find the good times and the bad, the joys and the pain that had made her who she was.

"HEY, KATIE!" Miles greeted her as he picked up the phone. "What's doing?"

"I heard you were back in town," said Cady warmly, suppressing the urge to tell him she'd been trying to reach him for over a week. "Kit tells me *Love and Regret* is a going concern again. Congratulations."

Miles shrugged. "Oh sure," he said, because it wouldn't do to let anyone know how worried he had been. "Sure, it always was. So, I want to talk to you. I want to see you."

Cady's heart thudded. "Sure," she said. "I'll be back in Toronto on the seventeenth."

"Oh, you're not in town?"

"No," agreed Cady without further explanation, and waited. Thea might or might not be right about telling him where she was and why, but Cady didn't want to risk it.

To her relief he let it pass without curiosity. "So, what's this? The sixth, right? The sixth of December. Yeah, this is tough. I'm due back in L.A., let's see, the eighteenth—the nineteenth. That's Monday. And I'm looking to stay there right over Christmas. We want to get this casting sewn up while I'm down there. No way of you getting back in town before the seventeenth?"

Well, there was no hope for it. "No, Miles, I'm doing a show."

"Oh yeah? What are you doing?"

"Lady Macbeth."

"Hey, oh yeah, you're a real actress, aren't you? So what'll—"

She said, "Look, I could fly in Monday the twelfth, we're dark that day. And out again early Tuesday. Could you see me Monday afternoon?"

"I could see you," Miles admitted, "but, you know, Katie, we want a screen test, right?"

She held her breath. "We do?"

"Yeah, and that's pretty tight booking. Say listen, you doing anything special over Christmas?"

"I— No," she said. Cady never did anything special over Christmas. She had long ago learned that going to a friend's home caused more pain than it soothed. Now she avoided any family get-together during that loneliest of all seasons.

"So come down to L.A. with me on the nineteenth," he said easily. "You'll have a good time, you'll get to meet the people, you know? Charm them a little bit. And if things go all right, we can do your screen test right there."

"I— Miles—"

"Don't worry about money or anything; the studio will pick up the tab, Katie. It would be a big opportunity for you."

If things go all right, she added cynically. *And we all know what things you're talking about.*

She had always been going to be somebody, she thought, remembering the eight-year-old who had promised herself, "Someday I'll show them!" and all the other little Cadys who had taken the terrible present of being alone and unwanted and triumphed over it by promising herself the future. She thought of the small child, gasping helplessly in her bed, drenched with icy water and clenching her impotent fists, saying inside, *you'll be sorry! You'll be sorry someday!*

And she thought of Margery Simpson whom she had shunned and hurt, and whom she owed so much, and of the dream of standing in front of the whole world, holding her acting award and saying, "And I want to thank my foster mother, Margery Simpson. . . ."

"Miles, it sounds like a great chance," she said into the phone. "Thanks, I'd love to come."

"HEY, GREAT!" said Dee with a grin. "So you found her. Where the hell has she been hiding?"

"I don't know that yet," Luke admitted. "I need you to track her down for me."

Dee sighed. "I shoulda known. All right, how am I gonna do that?"

Luke cleared his throat. "She was in a television commercial last night. I want you to tell me how to track through the production companies and ad agencies to find out her name."

Dee moved his lips out and in. "Okay," he said, picking up a pencil. "What's the product?"

"Hair shampoo," said Luke.

Dee grinned. "The name, Romeo. The brand-name."

"Oh!" said Luke. "Oh, ah, you know the stuff—" He stopped, looking blank. "Hell, one of those famous ones, I think. . .oh hell," he finished disgustedly. "I don't even know if I noticed the product name."

"Sounds like a great ad," Dee observed dryly.

"It was," said Luke. "Incredible ad."

"Except you didn't have a product association," Dee pointed out. "Oh, well, give it time. You know what time it played, what channel?"

"Yeah," said Luke. "What good will that do?"

Dee waved a hand. "Phone the station and ask them

who ran a shampoo last night at that time," he said.
"You know, Luke, I gotta tell you—I think this broad is
bad for you, man. You are just not firing on all cylin-
ders."

"Yeah, yeah, I know," agreed Luke. "When I do find
her I may just kill her. So what do I do—I phone the station? And they'll tell me?"

"They'll tell you," agreed Dee, laughing inordinately.

"You really have to do it?" asked Shirley sadly. "It
just doesn't seem right to me, Cady."

"Well, it's the way of the world," Cady told her as she
moved back and forth between closet and dresser and
the suitcase on the bed. "The way of my world, anyway."

Shirley's shining brown hair fell away from her ear as
she put her head on one side. She had grown up plain,
but the kindly light in her eyes and the warmth of her
own contentedness gave her face the glow of beauty.
She loved people, and so people loved her.

"Are you telling me that nobody ever got a part in a
movie without sleeping with the director?" she demanded.

"No— I don't know." Cady shrugged. "Some do and
some don't, I guess. I'm one of the unlucky ones—except that there are about a thousand actresses in the
world who would give ten years of their lives to be in
my place."

"But Cady, you don't like it. You aren't those other
actresses—and you're not happy about this."

In the past three weeks Shirley and Cady had become
close, their childhood memories providing the frame-
work and the rest an attraction of opposites. For Shirley
was calm and content and full of the milk of human
kindness, and Cady at the moment was a soul as lost as
any of her children at the clinic.

"No one would be *happy* about it, Shirley," Cady said, throwing the last of her cosmetics into the carryon in a jumble. "It's just something you do if you want to get ahead."

She locked her cases and plunked them all on the floor while Shirley watched.

"Cady," she said at last, "life gave you a real bad start, and that's not fair. But Cady, you're not a helpless kid anymore. A lot of your life is in your own hands now. And you can choose, Cady. We all choose sometime. And you're reliving your childhood over and over, it seems to me. You should stop and take a look around, Cady. You need someone to love you more than you need a career right now. You need—"

Cady whirled. "Just don't tell me I need a husband and babies, Shirley, okay?" she hissed, surprising herself with the force of her anger.

But Shirley was undaunted. She sat calmly, without flinching under the blast. "Cady, you've got to stop running sometime," she said.

She drove Cady to the airport while bright sunshine glinted blindingly off the broad white fields of snow.

"It really is flat, isn't it?" Cady marveled. "It really is just like a table. You forget when you're away."

"Now, you keep in touch," commanded Shirley as they dragged her luggage to the check-in counter. "And don't forget me when you're famous."

Cady laughed. "I won't," she promised.

"And be sure to use your real name on the credits!" Shirley said. "You're not in England anymore. And here you're Cady to all your friends."

All her friends. She had more than she knew, Cady reflected with a tearful little smile. Her old high-school mates had turned out in large numbers, once the word had gone round. Even Donnie White had been there, a big, smiling man, a once-prosperous farm-equipment dealer whose business was likely to be one of the economy's victims. "But, hell," he'd told Cady, "something'll turn up. I'm not so old I can't start over, not like some."

He was married, of course—Don White was the marrying kind—and he was happy, except for the economy.

She had smiled at him, and at her memories of the young Cady, who might now have been the woman he turned to at night when the thought of his business and his outstanding loans woke him...if things had been different.

And if things had been different, she just might have been happy, Cady saw, because Donnie White was a kind and gentle man who lived by the simple rules: he was a good husband and father and a good provider....

And I'd still be me, Cady thought, surprised, and the thought troubled her, as though some great truth lay just out of reach in her mind. *I'd still be me, because it doesn't seem to matter much what you do in life....*

"Yes, I'm going to use my own name," she promised Shirley, and then Shirley hugged her, and the tears pricked behind her eyes. "Just as I did here."

"Good luck," smiled Shirley, her eyes wet, too. "Good luck with whatever you do, Cady, and...be happy."

"IT WAS ON AT NINE O'CLOCK," Luke said patiently. "It was for a shampoo, and there was a woman—a woman with black hair...."

"Just a moment," said the woman cheerfully. "We'll find that for you."

Luke drummed his fingers and shifted in his seat till he heard the receiver being picked up again.

"Okay, I'm afraid you have a bit of a problem," she began apologetically. "Unless you know the product manufacturer."

"No," said Luke. "No, I don't. What's the problem?"

"Well," she said, "we had five commercials running in that spot. Now one was for a snow blower, so that's out, and another for Xerox, so that's out. But three of them are only listed by manufacturer's name, not by product, and all three of those manufacturers, I'm pretty sure, have shampoos."

Luke sighed in resignation. "What are they?"

"Johnson and Johnson, Bardel and Revlon," she read out.

"And there's no way—"

"I'm sorry, I have no way of knowing what product was being run," she told him.

"Is there any way I could find out?"

"Well, the best thing would be, when you see it again, make a note of the product name."

Luke thanked her and hung up. "When I see it again," he muttered. "If I have to. . . ."

He dialed the phone. "Dee, you gotta do me this favor," he began without preamble. "There are three manufacturers it could be. You gotta find out—" He described the problem.

"You don't know what you're asking, Luke," Dee said in an exasperated voice. "You know different products in the same company can have different ad agencies, man. You gotta find out the agency. How're you gonna do that when you don't even know the product name? Phone up every agency and describe the ad? You'll never find it!"

"Dee—"

"Man, look, I understand your problem, but I am trying to put together a film here. I am scheduled to go on location January 2. Are you with me?"

"Dee, just tell me. Do I have to watch television till I find that lousy ad again? Is that what I have to do?"

Dee exhaled smoke into the phone.

"As soon as you know the product I can find her for you," Dee said reasonably.

Luke hung up the phone and gazed with mute hostility at the silent television screen. "I don't believe it," he muttered. "I do not believe it." He picked up the remote control from his brown-spattered white sofa. "Cady," he said darkly. "There is one good side to all this. I used to wonder what I was going to do about your damned husband. But now I know—if I can take on eight hours of TV a day, I can take on anything."

"YOU GOT BACK TO TOWN OKAY, Katie," Miles Davidson said. "So are you packed?"

"Yes, I am," she said. "I hope I've got the right clothes," and then she wished she hadn't said that, because she should be exuding confidence. "It is summery weather there, isn't it?" she amended.

"Yeah, it's warm," said Miles unconcernedly. "So you're ready to be picked up about four-thirty, right?"

"Right."

Cady hung up the phone and walked listlessly to the window. There was snow falling, a heavy, wet snowfall that was already threatening to tie up the streets. *Oh please,* she begged silently, *please don't let it tie up the air traffic. I couldn't make this decision again. Please just let me get it over with. The sooner I sleep with him the first time, the easier it'll be. I'll be used to it, and then it won't matter.*

She moved over to Thea's brown corduroy sofa and sank dispiritedly down on it. Suddenly she was remembering the last time she saw Luke Southam. *Oh, Luke,* she thought tiredly, running her hand over her forehead. *I don't think I'd have got myself into this mess if it weren't for you.* She laughed soundlessly and mirthlessly and reached for a cigarette and lighted it. She inhaled deeply and looked at the cigarette in her hand. *And I wouldn't be smoking again, either.*

Funny that one man could be simultaneously the cause of her going off with Miles Davidson and the reason why she looked forward to the prospect of the trip with such aching regret.

If Luke had loved her, really loved her—and she was suddenly remembering the perfume in his bathroom cabinet with a gut-wrenching immediacy—she would never have considered Miles Davidson's proposition. It was because she had felt so cheated. . . . Cady shook her head and drew comfort from the cigarette. No, it wasn't that simple. It was all confused, too confused. She reached out tiredly to butt the cigarette. She was so tired, too tired to think. And in Los Angeles the day would be three hours longer . . . or the night.

Cady lay back against the worn brown corduroy of Thea's sofa and lifted her feet up. *I mustn't sleep,* she told herself as drowsiness claimed her, *I mustn't fall asleep and miss Miles. . . .*

IT WAS FOUR O'CLOCK when Luke burst into Dee's office, barely in time to catch him. Dee was on his way out.

"I've got the name!" Luke shouted at him. "The product name! Satinesse, it's Satinesse!"

Dee had to laugh. "Congratulations, how did you do that?"

Luke made a face. "I caught it on a cooking show a couple of hours ago."

"I didn't know you were a chef, Luke." Dee grinned.

"No jokes, please. I've got the ad-agency name, too. I called around. Now all you have to do is call them and get her name."

Dee shook his head. "Luke," he said, "can I do it when I get back?"

Luke eyed him. "When are you getting back?"

"In a week or two," Dee promised easily. "And it won't take me—"

A grinning Luke grasped his wrist. "The sooner you phone, the sooner you'll get to your flight."

Dee exhaled in exasperation. "Look, Luke, you've got the agency name? So just call them yourself. You can—"

"I did call them. They won't give me her name. They say they can't give it out. I told them I was working for you, that you were interested in her. And they said you'd have to call; they got suspicious. So—"

Dee looked at his watch. "Listen, Luke, I have a lady waiting. . . ."

But he was only prolonging the agony, and Luke grinned again. "She'll wait a lot longer, boy, if you don't pick up that phone."

"You should be writing melodramas, Luke," said Dee darkly, shaking his head.

CADY WIPED THE ACRID SMOKE from her eyes and coughed on a sob. *Luke*, she was thinking again. *God, those dreams, those awful dreams, whatever they are—it's because of you they came back. It's because everybody I ever loved left me while I was sleeping and when I found I couldn't avoid sleep, I decided never to love anyone again. . . but I couldn't avoid loving you, Luke. And just when I learned I'd been living half a life, Luke, you left me, and I'm left living half a life again. But the footsteps know, they know I broke the rules, and they're not going to let me forget.*

She looked at her watch. Four o'clock. Another half hour and Miles Davidson would come and pick up her soul as casually as he picked up her suitcase; and how he would restore it to her was anybody's guess.

She tried to recall that last night with Luke to give her strength. That had been endurable, hadn't it? She had got through that on physical need alone; she had left her

soul out of the equation and come out of it unscathed.
Hadn't she?

But she had loved Luke even then, hadn't she?
Whether she allowed herself to know it or feel it, inside
she had loved Luke...and she had known that Luke
loved her. He might have been betraying her, and his
future wife as well; he might be totally rotten in his dealings with women, but he had at least loved her. The real
her—not the beautiful body that Miles wanted to pos-
sess for possession's sake, but herself.

And that was why she had come out of it unscathed.
Love had been present, and where love was present,
even if betrayal was also present, then—and how did
she know this so suddenly?—then sex was a giving and
receiving, not a using.

Why was that? Cady suddenly recalled Shirley's
warm, loving face, how something, some power, had
transfixed the plainness to shining beauty.

Was the transforming power love? And therefore sex
without love—any human transaction, perhaps, that
omitted love—was a destructive force? But sex the
worst of all—a travesty of a deeply loving act, the form
without the substance?

She knew it was so. As Thea had known it, and Shirley. And of course, Luke. Luke who had written himself
into prose so powerful that it had unlocked the icy door
she had closed against her love for him and called up the
love buried deep inside herself.

She remembered suddenly what she had learned that
night in Algonquin Park, lying beside Luke in the
darkness after they had made love. She had known then
that she could never go off with Miles Davidson. She
had known then that it would be destructive.

She must not betray that understanding. She must not
give herself willingly to such destruction. She heard it
like a burst of understanding inside her, and knew as

clearly as she had once before that nothing could ever be
worth what she had nearly done . . . .

"YES, THAT'S RIGHT, the Satinesse ad," said Dee impatiently. "Yeah, look, I have a plane to catch, and I want
to take this girl's name to L.A. with me. Could you—all
right, thanks."

His fingers drummed the tabletop as he eyed Luke.
"What a damned furore over something so simple. I—
Yeah!" he turned back to the phone. "Yeah, this is Miles
Davidson, the director. Look, all I want is her *name*, I'm
not going to rape her. Yeah, yeah—*what*?" He snapped
forward in the chair and his jaw fell open so that his
cigarette fell out of his mouth onto the floor. Luke was
transfixed.

"Could you spell that, please? No, the first name.
Yeah, Kate, huh? Just as it sounds. Kate Hunter.
Thanks—no thanks, I have her agent's name. Yeah,
yeah."

Dee sat with his head bent, his eyes fixed on the name
he had automatically penciled onto the notepad in front
of him while Luke eyed him fixedly.

"What's the matter?" he asked. "Is that her name—
Kate Hunter?"

Dee began to shake his head from side to side in helpless surprise.

"It isn't? What is it, her agent's name?"

"No, it's her, it's her, old buddy," Dee said, looking
up at last. Then he took a deep breath and leaned back
in his chair. "Luke, old friend, you just ain't gonna
believe this . . . ." began "Dee" Davidson.

FOUR THIRTY-EIGHT. He was late. It would be funny if he
was just stringing her along, if he'd never meant to take
her, had been satisfied just to know that he could.
Maybe he did that all the time, maybe there were a

dozen actresses in Toronto, all expecting to be taken to L.A. tonight. . . .

She wished she could have got him on the phone. The last thing she wanted was a face-to-face confrontation that, if Miles Davidson were a vindictive man, might permanently damage her career hopes.

In the silence of the snow-covered world the sound of a car door slamming was like a gunshot. Cady ran to the window, but the streetlights showed nothing except a trail of footprints through virgin snow that led to her front door.

She stayed there, looking out at the footprints through her reflection and the room's in the broad expanse of window, stayed without moving as she heard the footsteps approach up the stairs of the building, heard them stop outside her door.

Footsteps; but this time it was no dream.

The dread built in her as the knock sounded on the door behind her. "Come in," she called, and watched with fascination the reflection of the door opening, and the shadowy figure enter.

Cady took a breath. *Goodbye fame, goodbye Cady Hunter the Somebody*, she whispered inside, but it didn't hurt as much as it might. As Donnie White had said, "I'm not so old I can't start over, not like some."

"Miles," she said calmly to the reflection in the window, "I'm sorry, I've changed my mind. I'm not going with you."

10

In the doorway Luke froze for a count of two. Then he moved into the room and shut the door behind him. He leaned against it, unsure what to say to that stiff, frightened back of the woman across the room who thought he was Dee Davidson.

At last he said, "Are you sure about that, Cady? Really sure?"

"Yes, I . . ." Cady began, and then, as the sound of his voice sank in, she whirled to face the man who had come for her, the man whose face in the glass lay in shadow. When she saw him she went white to the lips.

"Luke," she whispered hoarsely. "Luke, how— Oh my God, not *now*, not you now!" Her voice rose protestingly, and even to her own ears sounded as though tears were choking her.

Aching, she turned back to the window. Oh God, this would be worse than anything, to have Luke here while she faced Miles Davidson, to have Luke know what she had agreed to do. . . .

She said on a choke, "Luke, will you leave, please? Would you just go away without asking questions? *Please*?"

He advanced a little hesitatingly into the room, until he was within the pool of light cast by the lamp and she could see his face in the glass. The sense of recognition stole over her again, and she was free to examine that face as long as she liked, without his knowing. His hair was touched with snowflakes, and his thick jacket was hanging open.

Below her, in the street, the car sat with its engine running, and someone inside was smoking a cigarette. Luke's footprints, solitary in the deep virgin snow, led from the car to the front door of the apartment building.

She looked at her watch. Four forty-three. If Miles didn't come in the next quarter hour, he wouldn't come at all.

Behind her Luke said, "Cady, I've been looking for you so long. I love you, Cady."

Oh, but you're a man, she told him silently. *When Miles walks into this room and you know what I was going to do you'll stop loving me, I know that much. And it won't do any good to remind you about Sharon, and what you did and would probably do again, to both of us.*

She would rather face ten Miles Davidsons than watch the expression on Luke's face change from love to disgust.

She wished she were dressed, not naked under her bathrobe. But after having made the decision not to go with Miles she had caught sight of herself in her bedroom mirror, tricked out in the chic, casual clothes she had hoped to impress L.A. in. And she had suddenly been disgusted with herself as much as if she had put on skintight trousers and five-inch heels for a walk along Gloucester Street: one way or another, she was dressing up her body to sell it.

She had stripped herself bare before she knew it, almost retching with the knowledge that she had gone so far down the road before understanding.

But now she was wearing a bathrobe over nothing, and a beautiful robe it was, soft and sexy, in the deep, rich poppy red that suited her coloring beautifully. It had a loose narrow collar around a neckline that, while it covered her breasts, was only fastened at the waist, where the robe was cinched in with a thousand gathers over a beautifully flowing skirt that reached to the floor. The sleeves were also very full, and cinched in at the wrist.

It was her "Amanda" robe. A theater designer had designed it for her to wear in the first act of *Private Lives*, but when he saw her in it onstage the director had shaken his head. "Too voluptuous," he decided—quite rightly, in Cady's opinion. So she had worn a white satin thirties robe from theater stock and had bought the red robe from the designer for the price of the materials. She had always loved it, but now she wished she were wearing anything other than this.

Well, it was better to run headlong into pain than to wait for it to come to her like the footsteps. Cady took a breath.

"Luke," she said, "I'm here waiting for a film director to come and pick me up. I was going to L.A. with him. I was going to sleep with him to get a part in his film."

Softly out of the shadows she heard, "I know."

Silence fell in the softly lighted room. At last she turned to him. "You know?" she said, stunned. "How do you know?"

"Dee's an old friend of mine," he told her, watching every flicker of expression that crossed her face avidly, like a prospector panning for gold. "He's down in the car waiting right now."

She blinked. "Dee? Who's Dee?"

Luke's brows moved together. "Dee Davidson," he said. "Miles Davidson."

Cady's eyes snapped wide. "Miles Davidson! He's your friend? He's—" she whirled "—he's down there in the car?"

"Waiting for you."

She froze. "I, uh...." Clamping her eyes tight, she shook her head. "I'm con— What are you doing here?"

He said evenly, "I'm here to tell you I love you. And I have a message from Dee. He's faking you."

"You— He's *what*?"

"Dee has no part to offer you anymore. He has cast three Canadian actors in supporting roles, and therefore filled his quota. His producers are insisting he use Americans in the leads."

She made a motion, instantly suppressed, to glance toward the window, then faced Luke coldly. "He's been lying to me all this time?"

"Not as far as I can make out. It seems that up to a day or so ago it was still up in the air. But they want to get the casting nailed down. He was under pressure and in the end they wouldn't wait any longer."

She couldn't believe a chance could pass by so quickly. Even now, when she had herself chosen to let it pass her by, she felt a hurtful sense of an opportunity missed, a sudden regret that she hadn't taken Thea's advice about Regina.

Stoically she said, "And he was going to take me along for the ride anyway?"

Luke said, "He told me it would do you good to be seen by people down there, that he could do your career a lot of good even if he couldn't get you the part. He thinks you're a terrific actress, Cady."

"As well as a terrific sex object?" she asked bitterly. Oh God, when would men stop using women? She turned on Luke in sudden hostility. "So why did he send you here to tell me all this?"

"He didn't, Cady. He didn't want me along at all. But he knew I'd kill him if—" He broke off and took a deep, calming breath. "Cady, I can't stop you doing what you feel you've got to do. It's your life. I—I haven't spoiled your chances with Miles, though it was touch and go there, because I wanted to beat him senseless. He's down there waiting, Cady, in his chauffeur-driven limousine and all the trappings of success. You've got—" he looked at his watch, then kept his eyes on his wrist as though he could not bear to watch her face "—two minutes to go down and get in the car. If you don't go, he'll go by himself, but he won't carry away any desire for revenge, I promise you that."

She looked at him curiously. "But why are you here?"

Luke shut his eyes briefly. "To do what I can to keep you with me," he said hoarsely. "I was going to— But I can't, Cady. It's got to be your choice. You've got to make your own decision."

"You or my career?" she asked in a high voice.

Luke shook his head. "The only decision you make here is whether to go with Dee or not. I love you, Cady. If after that you—you need me, I'll be here."

She snapped, amazed, "What do you mean, you'll be here?"

He gazed at her silently, letting her read the answer in his face.

She choked out, "You love me. You really love me that much."

Silence. Cady turned back to the window.

"Oh, Luke," she said sadly, and waved her hand in a helpless gesture. "You don't want me. I'm so screwed up, Luke. I don't even know what love is, do I?"

"Every creature on earth knows what love is, Cady," Luke returned quietly. "You've just never had enough of it. But I'll teach you all about love."

She dropped her head, blinking. "That's what I mean," she whispered. "You're so normal and loving, Luke, you should have someone who—who can give you as much as you give them. I run away, Luke. I'm no good at—at . . . ."

Luke looked at her, letting the silence grow between
them as her voice faded.

After a moment he slipped out of his warm coat and
tossed it on a chair, advancing one or two paces as he
did so. Then he said, "Cady, you have more love to give
than any thousand other women put together. You're
just afraid to let go of it. I'm willing to wait, Cady, I
promise you. I'm willing to wait."

Tears burned her eyelids, the old familiar response to
gentleness. "Why?" she asked hardly.

"Because I will never love any other woman," he said.
"You're my life, Cady."

"Luke," she said. "Oh, Luke." She seemed incapable
of anything more. Below her, the dark car was pulling
away from the curb. "What were you going to do, how
were you going to stop me going with Miles?"

He shook his head. "Hold you here by force, maybe,
kiss you, make love to you—deliver an ultimatum. I
don't know."

Smiling through the tears in her eyes, she turned and
looked at him. She said, "You would have won. You
won before you began, Luke. I was never going anywhere with Miles Davidson, though I thought I was. I
couldn't go with him even if you didn't love me, even if I
never saw you again. I unpacked half an hour ago.
This—" she held out her arm, touching the folds of red
velvet that covered it, and grinned at him "—is my
bathrobe. Did you think I was going to fly to L.A. in a
bathrobe?"

Luke's eyes were grave with hope, but his mouth tried
valiantly to smile. "It looks like a sexy dress to me," he
said, trying to make a joke out of it, and then he held
out his arms.

The tears were starting down her cheeks as she ran to
him, and he enclosed her almost fiercely in his embrace.

"Cady, what is it?" he asked her softly, cradling her

head against his broad chest. "Tell me what it is, and we'll fight it. Whatever it is, we can conquer it together. I love you, Cady. Tell me why you've been running away from me."

She trembled against him. "Don't you know?"

"I've made a few guesses," he said with a wry smile. "You're married, that was the first that came to mind— the first and the worst. But I know you're not married."

"No," she agreed, almost inaudibly. "How do you know?"

"You were going to go off with my friend Dee," he said. "I knew you too well to think you could do that if you were married." There was a tremor in his voice, and she wondered if he had really been so sure of that.

She sighed. "I couldn't do it married or unmarried. I just . . . couldn't make myself do it."

He pressed her closer. "I'm glad you couldn't," he said. "It would have been a worse hell than I think I could take, letting you go off like that. I think I'd have killed him."

She smiled sadly, wondering if his stand a while ago had been just words. "I thought you said you wouldn't stop me."

"I wouldn't have. But afterward—if it hadn't killed me, I'd have killed him."

She closed her eyes and pressed her face against his neck, wanting to comfort the pain she heard in his voice. "He's gone now," she said. "The car's gone."

"Yes," he said. "Tell me why you were running away."

Cady took a deep sighing breath. There was so much to explain, so much of what she felt was in confusion.

"Shall I tell you what my second guess was?" Luke

asked gently. He took her silence for consent. "I thought, maybe you're afraid of men? You've been in a lot of foster homes. Perhaps you had bad experiences with a foster father and you just can't face a permanent sexual relationship?"

She was stunned into silence, and after a moment he put his hand under her chin and looked down into her face. "Is that it, Cady?" he pursued gently. "You were so free and loving with me it's hard to believe. But I thought—maybe you hated me afterward. Did you, Cady?"

"No, Luke. I never hated you."

"You don't have to hide from me. If that's what it is, I'll wait, Cady. I'll wait as long as it takes. Because I need you. I need you on any terms."

She closed her eyes and he heard her breath stop in her throat. "What is it, love?" he asked. "What did I say? That I need you? Does that frighten you?"

What frightened her was how much she wanted his need, and what she would do when he no longer needed her. She said, trying to find a way out of confusion, "Are you and Sharon married yet?"

He was shocked rigid. "Are we—am I—*what*? Are you seriously asking me if I married *Sharon*? After meeting you? After what I told you?"

But she knew. She had known before she asked. Sometime after he came into her room she had known unconsciously that Luke had the same honor he assumed in her. If she had assumed it in him, would she have known sooner that he could not marry another woman after what had happened between them?

"Luke—"

"By God," he said darkly, "there've been times in the past two months when I didn't know whether I'd beat you or love you when I finally found you, but, boy, I think I know now! You took off, and hid from me, and you put me through hell because of *Sharon*? After everything I told you?"

That was unfair. He had told her nothing.

"Luke, you told me you loved her, that you wanted to marry her."

"The hell I did! I told you I was living with a woman and I was going to have to sort that out when I got home! That was why—"

"You never said a word about sorting things out, Luke. You told me that if it weren't for me you'd have married her!"

"Well? What's that mean, except that I was sorry I hadn't got the right to take you back with me then? Anyway, I was wrong. I wouldn't have married her. I might have agreed to, perhaps, but no way would I ever have made it to the altar. With or without you. I know that now."

She said, "And you told her that?"

"Lady," he said, "you take a lot of convincing." He was angry. "I told her that the night I got home from Algonquin, lady—after I sat three hours at that restaurant waiting for you!"

It was a new experience, seeing Luke angry. But anger didn't frighten her. She was used to anger. Cady put her chin up. "And?"

"And? She moved out! Did you think I'd change my mind because I couldn't find you?"

She pointed out, "Well, somebody's makeup was all over the bathroom the night you took me to your place."

"Yes, and a lot of it is still there, because Sharon keeps hoping that if she drops by every few days to pick something up, one day she'll get me to change my mind." He paused. "And that's another little hell I wouldn't have been put through if you were around! I kept telling her I was in love with you, but you weren't there! And I put myself through hell wondering why, imagining the worst things imaginable, and now you tell me I went through it because you didn't trust me enough to give me a chance to explain? Because you wouldn't believe?''

At the tone of his voice, suddenly, the fear was on her again. The fear and the knowing that she had lost him, that she was unwanted, that she was going to get hurt. And all the defenses against loving that she had so painstakingly dismantled over the past few weeks began to tumble back into place. Cady drew away from him, twitching her robe more securely around her.

"I told you I wasn't the forever kind," she told him stiffly.

It stopped Luke dead. All his anger left him, and he stood looking at her, an odd light in his eyes. "You did, huh?" he said. "And I told you I *was*." He was watching, watching. "And I didn't hear any complaints."

A hand reached out and he pulled her against him, and the anger hadn't left him, it had been transmogrified into desire. "I told you," his voice was softly caressing, as one strong hand threaded its way into her hair, "that you were my mission in life, remember? My mission is to make you trust me, turn you into the forever kind, a one-man woman." He smiled meaningfully. "With me as the man."

His hands were so strong on her, in her hair and on the soft flesh of her upper arm through the thick silkiness of the velvet robe. The way she had never been held, had always needed to be held. She relaxed from stiffness, and her mouth opened on a small sigh. He saw his advantage.

"You've never been touched enough, remember?" he said in a low, whispering voice that rubbed along her nerves as his hands caressed her body—her back, arms, face, waist, buttocks and legs. "I'm the man who's going to touch you forever."

Her flesh and her heart rose to his touch, and she began to whimper with all the bruising need of the deprived child who still lived within. How strange that the fulfillment of all her need could make her heart ache so desperately, she thought dimly, could bring to the surface all the tears that the child had kept hidden, that the child had never let fall.

They began to fall now, the tears of anguish and need and yearning, and that terrible, automatic fear of the future rose up behind with tremendous force, so that in a moment Cady was gasping with sobs.

"It's all right," he promised softly, stroking her, kissing her gently as if she were indeed a child, and then he bent and slipped a hand under her knees, and lifted her up in his arms. "It's okay to cry, my love, it's okay." He moved to the sofa and sat down with her, still holding her tightly. "You can cry to me, Cady," he said, "I'll aways be here. I love you, Cady, my darling, my love, I will always be here." And somehow it made her cry more violently than ever, not because she did not believe him, but because she did. The tears that she wept now were the tears that one sheds when it is safe to weep; the tears of the person who was lost and who is found, of the exile who has come home at last.

She cried for the mother and father she had scarcely known, and for her empty heart and the long barren years of being afraid to love. She cried for the child who had learned to understand that death and loneliness were the price of loving, and for all her nights and days of knowing she was alone forever.

She cried in the release of knowing those days and nights were over, that Luke was the secret friend who had somehow been there since before she was born and would be there till the day she died. The husband, lover, father, brother, son who had been waiting for her to step into the stream of life where they could find each other.

Throughout it all he held her and told her he loved her and let her cry it out. And when it was over he dried her eyes and wiped her face and smiled lovingly at her.

"My forever woman," he said.

LATER, MUCH LATER, he kissed her gently on the lips and said quietly, "I want to make love to you now. I need you, Cady."

Cady nodded and stood up and led him to her bedroom. At the door they both stopped and eyed her narrow cot, then looked at each other out of the corners of their eyes.

"A single sleeping bag is one thing," Luke said with a slow grin. "But a man could get seriously damaged falling out of a thing like that!"

Cady laughed. He always made her laugh. "Your place?" she suggested softly.

"My place," agreed Luke. "Let's go."

He turned. She said, "Wait, wait—I have to get dressed!" and he eyed her appreciatively up and down.

"Waste," he muttered. "Sheer waste."

"Maybe." Cady smiled slowly at him, a smile he had seen before, in the commercial: the smile of a woman who knows her sexual power. "And maybe not."

She had probably never smiled at anyone like that in her life, other than onstage, but he had said he loved her and said he wanted her and she believed him.

He reached out an arm and pulled her to him almost involuntarily. "Lady, you be careful with those smiles," he warned her in a deep voice, and his other hand pushed her chin up so that her mouth was an offering to his.

He took the offering, deeply and thoroughly, then lifted his lips. "Just what does 'maybe, and maybe not' mean?" he growled.

She laughed as his desire communicated itself to her,

like a small electric shock tingling along her skin. "You'll see," she said. Luke had never seen her in anything pretty, anything delicate or feminine. Whenever he had made love to her she had been wearing jeans, or her old track suit. She wanted him to see her in lace and nylon, and she told him so.

Luke looked down at the red velvet robe, warm against pale skin, slightly open between full, beautiful breasts and outlining the length of her legs as she moved. His eyes kindled.

"This is pretty damn sexy, you know," he informed her. His hands found the knot of the belt at the same time as his sensuous, seeking lips breathed delicately against the curve where shoulder met neck. "I don't think I've ever wanted to take anything off a woman in my life the way I want to take this off you."

He pulled the knot and the robe opened to the pale velvety flesh of her breast and leg, and the suddenness of his desire shook her so that the flicker of his eyes was like a touch. "We could make love on the floor, Cady," he whispered temptingly into her ear. "Cady, Cady, I need you, I've never needed...."

She moved uncomfortably against the desire that rose in her blood. "Thea might come home, she comes at odd times. Please—" She didn't know how to say that she didn't want to share even the tiniest knowledge of their love with anyone else. Not yet. Not while it was so new she hardly knew it herself. "Please could we go to your place, Luke?" And he smiled and understood.

"If I call a taxi, will you be ready by the time it gets here?"

She looked out the window. In this weather a taxi would take at least half an hour. "You got it," she said, pushing him out of the bedroom and shutting the door behind him. "There's probably some plonk or some

Scotch or something in the kitchen. Help yourself to what you want," she called.

The door opened, and her eyes snapped up. "Luke, you—"

"What I want isn't in the kitchen," he told her. "It's in here."

Laughing, she pushed him out again, then flew to the bureau, pulled out some bits of cotton and lace, and began to dress.

She hummed as she moved about the room, trying this or that piece of clothing, putting up her thick hair, checking her stockings and makeup; she hummed a strange, almost tuneless little hum that was the music of happiness, of a heart completely free.

"How do I look?" she demanded, pirouetting for his appraisal in the living room when she had finished. She had put on a red cashmere dress in the same deep poppy red as the velvet robe. It was her color, a shade that looked startling against her pale skin and black hair, startling and voluptuously beautiful. Like the robe, too, the dress opened down the front, buttoning from a vee deep between her breasts to the slightly below knee-length hem. Unlike the robe, however, the soft, silky smooth wool of the dress hugged her body, outlining the fullness of her breasts, her small waist and the womanly curve to her hips.

Only the sleeves were wide and full, like those on the robe, caught in delicately at slim wrists, where a tiny gold chain bracelet glinted.

At the base of the vee between her breasts was just visible the delicate lace of underwear—just enough to make a man wonder what the lace might be attached to; and she had left the bottom buttons open to just far enough above the knee that the flash of nylon stocking tantalized with every step she took.

There was another chain of thin gold glinting against

the skin of her neck, and two gold hoops in her ears. Her hair was stacked in a loose, casual style on her head, and held in place with combs.

Luke showed his teeth in a smile, and his blue eyes were navy with a look that made her breath catch in her throat.

"You look good enough to eat, and you damned well know it," he told her evenly. "Do you really want to go to my place, or can we just go back in there and I'll take them all off again? I'll risk the bed. I don't care how narrow—"

But Cady had heard the horn outside, and she brushed past him, wafting the scent of Femme as she moved to get her coat out of the hall closet. She had put on a pair of little black high-heeled boots that came up to fold over in a cuff just past her ankle. They would be useless in this weather, and the snow might well ruin the delicate leather, but she didn't care. She had never in her life before so wanted to entice a man, nor ever, in spite of her beauty, felt that she had the power to make a man lose his head. But just this once she would allow herself to feel it.

"You look so beautiful," Luke said in her ear when they were settled in the back of the taxi, close and warm and dark. "Would you like to stop off somewhere for dinner first?" He sat up a little straighter. "I've never taken you out to dinner, do you realize that?" He looked at her, and suddenly the memory of Hunter's restaurant was between them—his long, tormented wait, her panicked flight.

"Let's not talk about that," she whispered close to his cheek and neck, wishing for the power to drive the memory out of his mind.

As if in automatic response to the silken touch of her breath his hand came up to cup her head, and he turned to catch her lips with his. "If you keep doing that," he

whispered, "we won't be going anywhere except straight
to bed."

Cady looked at him under long lashes for a moment.
Then she turned her head and deliberately pressed her
face into his neck and blew another gentle breath there.

He made an involuntary move toward her, as though
they were attached to each other by wires and she had
pulled on them. "Witch," he whispered in her ear, sending little electrical pulses through her whole body.
"What will the driver think?"

She turned her lips to his ear and whispered back, "If
there's any justice in the world, she'll probably think
you're a fallen man."

Luke jerked his eyes around in surprise, but Cady was
right: that long hair didn't belong to an aging hippy, but
to a woman. Luke began to laugh. "I'll sacrifice my
reputation if you'll sacrifice yours." And he bent and
kissed her with a deep hungry urgency that belied the
casual laugh.

There was a light burning over the door of the house
when the taxi pulled up, and the big front window
glowed with the warmth of a lamp within. As they
pushed open the wrought-iron gate Cady stopped short,
pulling on his arm.

"What is it?" said Luke, concerned.

She was standing, staring at the house, at the warm
glow of light spilling out onto the snow. His voice startled her into awareness. She shook her head.

"Nothing," she said. "Nothing's wrong. It's—it's very
pretty, that's all."

He knew there was more, but he didn't push. "Come
inside," he said instead, unlocking the door. "It's cold
out here. Come in and get warm."

Luke shook off his sheepskin-lined jacket and hung it
on a brass hook beside the door, then took Cady's coat
and hung it up. The air was warm and the house very

cozy, with no drafts of chilling air, Cady discovered as she moved around. She slipped off her delicate little boots and picked them up to carry them into the kitchen after Luke.

"Have you got a cloth I could use to wipe these?" she asked. "Between the salt and the snow they'll be ruined."

Luke was filling the kettle. "Mrs. Markle must have them around somewhere," he said musingly. He plugged the kettle in. "Let's look under the sink." He suited the action to the words and passed her a cloth, then stood watching her as she deftly cleaned the boots.

She felt the focus of his attention, his energy on her, and became suddenly aware of how much masculine tension lay behind that gentle, patient exterior. He was wearing a black turtleneck that molded his chest and arms and the strong column of his throat, and wool trousers in a soft brown color that looked comfortably loose.

Not a man who felt the need to advertise his deep sensuality, she realized dimly. Or perhaps it was simply that living with a woman meant that he did not need to.

As though he had picked up on the thought, Luke said quietly, "We don't have to keep this house if you feel uncomfortable here. I've had it for five years, Sharon was here for only the last two, so it's not linked inextricably with her in my mind. But I don't mind selling it if that's what you want."

Cady put her cleaned boots down on the floor. "I. . .I don't know," she said. "I mean—are you asking me to move in with you?"

"Would you marry me?" he asked abruptly.

She was shaken to the core.

"I know you don't like the idea much," he continued quickly, seeing the look on her face. "I don't want to pressure you, Cady—I wasn't going to say anything—

but suddenly I just wanted you to know that I want to marry you."

What a hold the world would have on her then, if she married Luke. Marriage. That was as good as broadcasting the information to Fate that you were vulnerable, that you could be hurt. Everyone she had ever loved had been taken away from her, as though her love was a curse. That was what she had always thought as a child, she remembered suddenly—that it was her fault her parents and grandparents had been killed. Because she had loved and needed them so much.

The people she most loved were the ones in the greatest danger. So if she loved someone she mustn't love them. The more she loved someone the more frantic she was to save them from her dangerous love.

If she married Luke and had his babies, how could she help pouring all her pent-up love on them . . . ?

Never before had this conflict been presented to her in such black-and-white terms. She had never before seen this terrible action that ruled her life, had only been driven mercilessly by it, only operated in direct response to its dictates.

Was this why she had run from Luke?

Cady gazed at his open, waiting face, breathing as heavily after that mental journey as if she had run up half a dozen flights of stairs.

"Luke," she whispered, "I'm so afraid. If I love you too much—"

She stopped, unable to put the unspeakable into words.

He smiled as though he were hurting. "You can't love me too much, sweetheart," he told her softly. "I need you to love me. I need all the love you've got."

"I'm cursed," she rasped, trying to make him understand. "Everyone I love dies, or leaves me." It sounded so strange, so ridiculous, put in words.

"I won't die, and I won't leave you," he promised.

If she said it all aloud, would the terrible charm be broken? Would everything seem as ridiculously unlikely as what she had just said?

She said, "Do you think someone's love could be a curse? That it could kill people?"

He was silent with shock. "No," he said. "*No.* Is that what you thought?" He swore violently. "Is that what you've told yourself all these years? It isn't true, Cady. I promise you it isn't true. Love is the only pure good in the world."

Yes, she had felt that, had understood it a few hours ago. Love was good. Evil was the absence of love.

Don't love him! warned the six-year-old Cady inside her, in a voice that had ruled her emotions for over twenty years. She could even remember suddenly, with diamond clarity, the terrible moment when she had first made the connection. *Don't love him!*

But a six-year-old child doesn't understand the simple rules of the world. She was twenty-two years older now, and sheer logic knew that the childish voice was wrong. She must break the child's irrational grip on her emotions. She must allow her adult understanding to undo all the knotted misunderstanding that stood in the way of her happiness.

She smiled slowly and a little fearfully at Luke. "I'll need help, Luke," she told him calmly. "And I'll need time. I know what I want now, but I've got to learn how to let myself take it."

Luke smiled in relief and admiration, and turned to pull out the plug of the almost-boiling kettle. "To hell with coffee," he said. "Do you want coffee?"

"No."

He strode over to her and bent to swing her up in his arms. "Let's start those lessons on how to take what you want," he said huskily.

HE SET HER ON HER FEET beside the big bed and began to undo the buttons of the red dress. His knuckles and fingers brushed her breasts and then down the long curve of her stomach as he worked, and she closed her eyes and he saw her breast heave in response. She was shivering under the lightest of touches, and he saw her nipples harden under the sensuously soft wool.

His hands began to tremble in response, and as he reached the buttons that hid her hips and thighs from him, his fingers fumbled with his urgency.

She was wearing only the lightest underwear underneath, only lacy knickers to match her pretty cotton camisole, and stockings held up by a delicate garter belt. His touch was as immediate against her as if she had been naked, and she looked down at his dark head as he knelt in front of her, and a soft moan of desire breathed from her.

"Luke," she said. "Luke."

Finally he undid the last button, the one midway between knee and hips, and she felt the delicate flesh of her thighs shiver violently under his touch.

Luke pushed aside the folds of the dress and then froze into immobility as he saw what she was wearing underneath.

"Woman, what are you trying to do to me?" he asked hoarsely. "Kill me?" He closed his eyes. "Cady, I haven't touched another woman besides you since Algonquin Park. This is too sexy, Cady, too... tempting."

Still kneeling, he stroked the flesh of her leg through the delicate nylon of her stocking, stroked her from ankle to thigh, then to the uncovered flesh above the stocking top.

"Cady," he whispered, and it sounded like prayer, "how I've dreamed of touching you, Cady—the feel of you, the woman scent of you. . . ."

He fingered the lacy garters, white against her silken

flesh, and breathed deeply to calm his hammering pulses. "Do you know how sexy this is?" he demanded roughly. "Do you have any idea what this is doing to me?" He pressed his face against her, and kissed her, and his mouth was hot against her tender flesh; even through the lace his touch burned her.

It was as though desire burst up simultaneously everywhere in her body; one moment there were a hundred tiny fires, in the next she was an inferno of need. Cady's knees buckled and she sank onto the bed. "Please, Luke," she whispered again. "Please."

Luke stood up, his blue eyes almost black as he gazed at her. In one quick motion he pulled the black sweater over his head and dropped it to the floor; then his hands moved to his belt.

She sat on the bed with her feet curled under her, watching breathlessly the movement of his hands.

Luke licked his lips and breathed heavily. "You'll drive me nuts, looking at me like that," he said hoarsely. "For God's sake, Cady—"

Her lips parted to take in a small breath then as his hands pulled the soft beige stuff of his trousers open and down. Underneath she saw a soft black cloth, and under that . . . .

He threw aside trousers, shoes and socks and stood for a moment looking down at her, and Cady suddenly found herself scrambling off the bed to him, kneeling to press her face against the black cloth, as his face had pressed against lace.

But he bent and his hands closed on her arms in a grip of steel. "No," he rasped. "No, dammit, Cady, I'm going to go out of control in a minute. Stop. Cady, sto—"

A tremendous emotion surged through him as he bent and picked her bodily off the floor and carried her to the bed. He sat down beside her and kissed her with the wildest passion she had ever known. His hungry hand pressed her arm and then her full breast under the delicate silk.

One handed, he wrestled to undo the buttons, and finally was able to thrust the white silk apart to expose the whiteness of her breast and the hard, dark, expectant beads underneath.

He closed his eyes. "Cady," he said. "I can't wait any more. I want you now, Cady, my woman, my love, I want to be inside you."

Without a word she pulled off the last bits of nylon and lace that kept him from her and lay back looking at him. "I want you, too, Luke," she whispered. "Please don't wait, please don't make me wait."

Her heart was aching with the depth of her need, and she could not tear her eyes away from him as he took off the black cloth and was naked at last to her view.

He rose up over her and settled into the cradle of her hips. He said, "You're the sexiest, most beautiful woman I've ever known. Your need shows in your eyes, did you know that? There's never been a woman who looked at me the way you look at me."

His body was hard against her, so hard and urgent she felt faint. Her breathing was a series of small moans as he lifted his hips and pressed against her, demanding entry.

Her body admitted him with a sweet aching, a sense of completion and perfection, as though truly they became one flesh. Cady sighed a honeyed sigh as she fell down and down into a deep realm of darkness where pleasure reigned, and all the senses—sight, smell, hearing, taste and touch—brought in their treasures for its sole use.

The salty, soapy taste of Luke's flesh; the sight of his darkened eyes above her, avidly watching her face for every trace of his power over her; the sound of his voice and his breathing and the gentle slap of flesh meeting flesh; the masculine scent of Luke's skin; and above all the deep tingling, thrilling thrust of his body against her flesh—all these were taken in and added to the growing urgency in her that told her that only too much was enough.

When Luke's eyes clenched shut and his breath began to escape in moans she felt her body begin to lift against him, felt her hands cling demandingly to his shoulders, his back, his hips; felt the tight knot of pleasure that had been slowly building in her begin its fast unwind.

It caught her on the first spin. "Luke!" she cried out in high surprise. "Luke, oh my God, Luke..." as the urgency blazed a trail through all her veins and pleasure followed after, its honeyed sweetness coursing to the ends of her being.

"I love you, Cady," Luke was saying, over and over, as pleasure took its clenching hold on him and shook him—the pleasure she had given him, making him shudder and tremble and cry her name and his love over and over.

CADY STOOD AT THE MIRROR, pulling the few remaining pins out of her tangled hair so that it tumbled down her back.

Luke, lying on the bed watching, said lazily, "You could sell me anything, doing that."

"I could— Oh! My commercial! Did you see it?"

"If I hadn't, we wouldn't be here."

She smiled inquiringly at his image in the mirror.

"Would you mind telling me why you aren't in *Face to Face with Talent*?" he asked by way of explanation.

"Oh, the Canadian talent book! Well, because I've been working in England for the past six years."

Luke muttered darkly.

"*What* did you say?" she demanded.

He said, "Nice of you to tell me. Do you know how

many times I looked through that damned book for your face?"

"You should have been looking in *Spotlight*," she told him carelessly, picking up a brush. "That's the English book."

Luke looked at her. "Careful," he warned gently. "I have a frayed temper these days." But there was a note of honeyed postlovemaking satisfaction in his voice that belied the words. "It is especially horrible to remember all those photographs and résumés of Dee's I went through."

"Well, I would be among those, that's for sure," Cady said.

"You might have been, if you hadn't been up for a part in *Love and Regret*. As it was, you, along with all the others he was considering, were in his damned briefcase!" When he had learned that this afternoon, Luke had nearly killed Dee Davidson in sheer temper.

Cady laughed in commiseration. "Oh no! So you had to give up the search? And then what? You happened to see me on that commercial? That was luck," she observed, enjoying the pull of his brush through her thick hair making her scalp tingle.

"It was no luck," Luke said firmly, "and I did not give up. I have been to more shows and parties in this town, and watched more bloody television!"

"Parties?" she said. "What did parties have to do with it?"

"I thought you might be at a theatrical party or hangout. I made Dee take me to anything that was going."

Cady gurgled. "Oh gosh—and all the time I was out of town."

"You weren't!" he declared disgustedly. "Were you? Damn, all those smoky crowded places—where were you?"

"In Regina, playing Lady Macbeth with the Old Foundry."

He looked at her. "Regina," he said in sudden understanding. "And how was that?"

"Strange," she said, knowing that he wasn't asking
about the play. "Hard. I went back to as many old
places and found as many old faces as I could." She
looked at him. "You somehow started something in
me—I had to see it through."

Luke smiled gently. "It takes a brave person to do it
on her own. I wish I'd been with you." And she thought
of the pain of standing under the ghost of the maple tree
and remembering, and wondered if her eight-year-old
self would have been comforted by Luke's presence, and
if thirteen-year-old Cady would have approved of
Luke...yes, it would have been easier, much easier,
with Luke to help and hold and remind her that those
days were over.

"Did you find your foster mother?"

"Margery?" she asked. "No, though I tried. I even
phoned his firm in Vancouver, and asked around in the
old neighborhood, but no luck."

Luke said, "We'll find her together, shall we?" and her
heart missed a beat.

"How?"

"There are ways. They'll have left a trail—they
weren't deliberately trying to disappear, were they? So a
detective, if it comes to that, will find them."

Suddenly she knew that she had to do it. If she was
going to understand herself she had to meet the good
parts of her past as well as the bad. Margery Simpson
was the only mother she had, the only one whom she
really remembered.

"I want to find them," she said.

Luke grinned. "I wish I'd thought of you having gone
to hunt down your past. I might have found Margery
Simpson already, and I'd a darn sight rather have been
talking to her than watching television!" He sighed.

"Well, at least it's over. I never have to watch that thing again as long as I live."

"Oh, yes, you will," Cady contradicted him with a grin. "You'll have to watch my shows, and you'll have to come to my opening nights and the parties after-ward...." Luke groaned, and Cady laughed. " 'Course, in return, I expect to read all your manuscripts."

"Why don't we combine those?" Luke suggested.

"Yes?"

"I'll write screenplays for you to star in."

She put the brush down and walked over to sit beside him on the bed. "Well, I like the part you've written for me so far." She smiled a small courageous smile.

Luke was still, watching her as though the smallest motion might destroy the confidence he had worked to create. "What part?" he asked as though he knew, but wanted to hear her say it.

"Your woman," she said softly, "your...wife?" And his hand buried itself in the thick cloud of her hair and pulled her face down for his kiss.

"LUKE, YOU'VE GOT a cupboard full of Oreo cookies!"

"I have?" his muffled voice came from the depths of the fridge.

"There must be three, four, five—*six* packets in here. What on earth do you do with all those cookies?"

"I eat 'em," he said. "Look, I've found two frozen piz-zas. How about that?"

"You *eat* them! Six packets? At a time?"

"Well, when I have writer's block, they help me find my ideas. And here's some frozen chips, and a pie!"

"Junk food," she observed, shaking her head. "Do you only eat junk food?"

"I like it," he said defensively. "Anyway, at least I don't smoke."

Cady gulped guiltily. "That was because of you," she

told him. "I haven't smoked since I was twenty, but I had to calm my nerves somehow."

"Well, now you've got me, could you quit again? I think Oreo cookies are a lot healthier. Even frozen pizzas are healthier. Even Coke is healthier."

"All right, I'm a fraud. So I'll quit. Satisfied?"

Luke eyed her up and down as she stood in the middle of his kitchen floor, wrapped in his big blue bathrobe. It matched her eyes, as it matched his.

He said, "Our kids will all have black hair and blue eyes, just like us."

"They will?" she faltered.

"Have you never thought that the best way to make up for having no family is to create one?"

"I. . . ." Her voice dried up and she tried again. "There are so many unhappy, lonely children in the world, Luke. Would we have to make our own? Couldn't we. . . adopt some children?"

Luke nodded slowly, considering the idea for the first time. "Yeah," he said thoughtfully. "Yeah, why not? If we can stop someone suffering what you had to suffer. . . ."

The shadow of the eight-year-old Cady who still stood under the maple tree on a summer street and heard them call, "orphan" and "bastard" and "no one will ever adopt her," was comforted at last.

"We'll give them lots of love, won't we, Luke?" she said, feeling tears prick her eyelids as her love for him overflowed.

"Yes," he agreed. "We'll give them all the love they need—but not right away, Cady. First I want to give you the love *you* need. You're my mission in life, remember?"

"I remember." She smiled at him through tear-spangled lashes.

Luke threw the frozen chips and pizzas onto the counter and closed the fridge, then crossed to take her in his arms. "I want to fill you up with love," he said, kissing the top of her head as she buried her face in his warm comforting chest. "Let's wait a few years before we decide anything, okay? You have a lot to catch up on."

She smiled through her tears and reached up to kiss him. "Right now I have to catch up on two missed meals. Are you going to put those awful pizzas in the oven?"

"*Awful!*" he repeated, stunned. "Those are McCain's Frozen Pizzas, you know! Awful! They're the crème de la crème of pizzas! Don't you know anything at all about hot cuisine?"

Cady looked at him. "I suppose you think I'm walking into that one," she said dryly.

He had the grace to laugh. "Oh, well, anything's worth a try."

He cooked the pizzas but not the chips, and they sat in the living room, watching the news as they ate. Afterward, Luke shut off the television, put his empty plate to one side and stretched.

"Ah," he said, looking the picture of the satisfied male. "Love and food, the two great sensual experiences of life, and both in one day."

Cady was looking down at the sofa seat. "Luke," she said, "there are a whole lot of little brown polka dots on your sofa. I've never seen anything like it."

"Neither has my cleaning lady," he muttered under his breath, looking at the top of her unsuspecting head as though he were suddenly remembering the entire catalog of her sins.

"Is it supposed to be like that? Or what caused it?"

Luke grinned at her. "You know what?" he said. "I forgot the third great sensual experience of life."

"Yeah?" she asked curiously as he reached for her.

"Yeah," he told her. "And I'll bet you're curious about

what the third great sensual experience of life is, aren't you? You bet you are," he added without pausing. "Well, I'll tell you. The third great sensual experience of life—which tonight may include elements of both the first two—"

"Great sensual experiences of life," she said with him.

"—is revenge."

She looked up from her home against his chest. "What?" she faltered.

"Yes," said Luke. "And boy, do you owe me revenge. You owe me for my broken lamp, and my polka-dot sofa and my missed deadlines and— Oh, the list is endless."

"And you're going to get that revenge, how?" she demanded with a challenging smile.

Luke slid an arm under her knees and around her back, stood up and headed for the stairs. "I'll think of something," he assured her. "It may take me all night, but I'll think of something."

"Now, Luke, don't—" she began with a grin. He smiled down at her until both their smiles faded and they were both breathing too quickly.

"Cady," he told her, "don't say don't."

EPILOGUE

"A WHITE CHRISTMAS," Cady said happily, her arm in the crook of Luke's, her hand enclosed in the warmth of his and tucked into his big pocket. With their other hand each of them carried a shopping bag full of gifts as they walked along the quiet, snowy street from the car.

Outside the house, Cady stopped and looked. It was dark, and there was silence all around, and stars twinkled in the black sky and from the shiny surface of the thick snow.

It was a big house, a modern suburban house that looked inviting and comfortable. In the window the lights of a Christmas tree flashed on and off, and against the white door under the welcoming light hung a large red-and-green holly wreath.

Light spilled from the main window out onto the snow while upstairs the windows were dark. Everyone would be downstairs, grouped around the tree. If she stood very still and listened, she could hear laughter, and voices singing "It Came Upon a Midnight Clear."

"Oh, Luke, look," she said, breathless with a choking emotion.

"Yes," he said, alerted by her tone. "Yes, Cady, what do you see?"

She said, "Luke, your brother's house, the way it looks; that's the way houses have always looked to me—so cozy and welcoming, and light coming from the window. It's always been the symbol of what other people had that I could never have. Always, always, I've been on the outside looking in."

"Cady," he whispered, his heart torn in two by the note he heard in her voice.

"I've never belonged anywhere, Luke," she said, and her cheeks in his line of vision glistened with tears as she gazed at the beautiful, welcoming house. "Never, until now. I belong to you now, don't I, Luke?" she was smiling and crying together. "I even belong with your family, don't I?"

"Yes," he said. "You belong, Cady. You belong to me, and you belong in the family, and you always will, my love. You belong with us all."

And she belonged in that house. She would go inside that pretty, inviting house and she would be welcomed by his family—*her* family—as someone who belonged there, belonged in the light and the laughter and the music of rejoicing; and in the bustle and the smell of baking, and in all the things that she had always known a home should have. She would even help to make the noise and the laughter, and the wonderful smells of cooking; she would help make the joy, the way she had always yearned to do.

And a passerby might look up at the window of the house, and hear the sounds that the happy house enclosed, and button up more warmly and hurry more quickly to his own home.

But the small child that stood on the outside, cold and lonely for so many years, would be cold and lonely no longer. She did not belong on the outside now. As Cady and Luke moved up the snowy front walk and the door was opened to them, a small invisible child detached herself from her station in the shadows and slipped in behind them.

"Cady! Luke!" a smiling voice greeted them. "Merry Christmas! Come in, it's cold out there! Come on in where it's warm!"

And they did.

THE AUTHOR

Alexandra Sellers grew up in more than half a dozen small towns across Canada. The experience must have put travel into her blood, because she's spent much of her adult life trying to absorb as many languages and cultures as her budget allows. Another of Alexandra's passions is reading—and writing—fiction. "Once you've discovered the world of books," she says, "you're as free as your own imagination."

Books by Alexandra Sellers

HARLEQUIN TEMPTATIONS
6—THE FOREVER KIND

HARLEQUIN SUPERROMANCES
13—CAPTIVE OF DESIRE
42—FIRE IN THE WIND
87—SEASON OF STORM

These books may be available at your local bookseller.

For a free catalog listing all titles currently available, send your name and address to:

Harlequin Reader Service
P.O. Box 52040, Phoenix, AZ 85072-2040
Canadian address: Stratford, Ontario N5A 6W2